MW00966520

A city suburb, 1980. The front of propriety, the freakish stillness and the bush parties. This is the home of Germaine Stevens, a social misfit who thinks she's struck ultimate cool when she's accepted into her preppie high school's only counter-culture group, the Rockers. Yet has she really just traded one kind of conformity for another? And is she still a loser?

Her friends are desperate characters: Regina's on the road to ruin, Bono's more boy than girl, and Jackie's postering her bedroom into a rock 'n' roll tomb. Yet beneath the party-hardy attitude, no one is as disaffected as they seem, or want to be.

In a voice that ranges from tough to achingly vulnerable, Sharon English powerfully conveys the anger, lust and absurdity that spiral into one girl's growing fight against the tuned-out numbness of her world.

# UNCOMFORTABLY

# numb

## Sharon English

*Kathleen —*

*With thanks and looking forward*
*to more words.*

*Sharon English.*

The Porcupine's Quill

NATIONAL LIBRARY OF CANADA CATALOGUING IN PUBLICATION DATA

English, Sharon, 1965–
 Uncomfortably numb / Sharon English.

ISBN 0-88984-250-7

I. Title.

PS8559.N5254U53 2002     C813'.6     C2002-904168-6
PR9199.4E54U53 2002

1  2  3  4  •  04  03  02

Published by The Porcupine's Quill,  www.sentex.net/~pql
68 Main Street, Erin, Ontario  NOB ITO.

Represented in Canada by the Literary Press Group.
Trade orders are available from University of Toronto Press.

We acknowledge the support of the
Ontario Arts Council, and the Canada
Council for the Arts for our publishing
program. The financial support of the
Government of Canada through the
Book Publishing Industry
Development Program is also
gratefully acknowledged.

ONTARIO ARTS COUNCIL
CONSEIL DES ARTS DE L'ONTARIO

Canadä

The Canada Council | Le Conseil des Arts
for the Arts | du Canada

For the girls, back then, who wouldn't shut up

# Table of Contents

Monsters  11

Stories  21

A Short Chronicle of Tenth-Grade Love  41

Thaw  61

Clear Blue  79

Heirlooms  97

The Academic Adviser  117

Bread and Stones  135

A Dirty Little Secret  155

Evolutions  173

Things become familiar without your getting used to them.

— JOHN BERGER, *To the Wedding*

# Monsters

Fuck 'em if they can't take a joke.

'Whoo-hoo!' we holler on the way to school. Three of us hogging the snow-packed sidewalk so the public schoolers get ploughed aside, teetering over boot-holed mounds. Friday morning: a fresh pack of smokes zipped in my pocket with five bucks for tonight's stash and my hair's getting long again, almost touching my shoulders after that Dorothy Hamill disaster Mom talked me into for graduation. 'Yahoo!' I shout, and pounce in the path of a grade fiver.

'Hey kid, wanna buy some acid?'

Jackie and Bono pissing themselves. The freaked-out girl mumbling 'No, thank you' and beelining for safety, woolly pom-pom bopping on its string as she flails through a thigh-high drift – it's better than cartoons. So good that we get on a roll propositioning all the other kids. A few can take it, crack 'I've already taken some!' or 'Not from *you.*' These are the kids who aren't yet hopeless. To the pop-eyed rest, we're clearly monsters. Black shapes looming on the sidewalk, howling in the swirling snow, threatening to crash into their soda-pop lives.

Jackie and I listen to *Houses of the Holy* and *Their Satanic Majesties Request* in her room. Not long ago, Jackie probably

......................................................................

wouldn't have figured out that her mom's having an affair.
Clued-out kids. We hunted through our parents' dresser
drawers and found vibrators and birth control pills, but that
was no big deal, your parents having sex. It didn't make us
pay attention.

Jackie's room used to be white and airy. The rose-
patterned wallpaper with its Scotch-tape scars still peeks
between posters and magazine cut-outs. Mrs Black never
comes in, just hollers from the landing or drops the laundry
basket and vacuum outside the door. Jackie tells me I should
make the same arrangement with my mom. But my parents
are angry now that they've seen my first-term grades, so I
have to be careful what I push for.

'You're in the doghouse, Germaine,' said my brother Ian,
smirking. 'Only six months of high school, and already
you're in the doghouse. At least you've got the hair for it.' A
total stoner, but guess who's acting like Mr Morality now he's
got his diploma? My grade print-out a column of C's. 'What
happened?' My parents gaping, hovering in my bedroom
doorway on the edge of this strange new space I've been
twisting from the old: lace curtains knotted, bed legs gone
and the light bulbs too, replaced with 25-watt reds. Gaping
wide-eyed with dumb worry, like children whose favourite TV
program's been cancelled. *What's happened?* They flip the
channels but the show's gone. I shrugged. Dad got angry. 'Pay
attention!' But I am. What he meant was, Be like you were
before.

Mrs Black's having an *affair*. I say this word in my head.
Poking my potatoes at the supper table, during the drone of
history and biology and math, I try to connect *affair* to report
cards. To creased trousers and wedding bands. To vacuum

cleaners and laundry baskets, shovelled driveways with brittle
Christmas trees left curbside, still fluttering tinsel, and the
pale glow of lawn lamps in the silence of our street after dark.
Mrs Black goes to her affair in her car before Mr Black comes
home from work. She leaves casseroles on the stove and
claims she's meeting a girlfriend for coffee or a drink if
anyone asks. Yeah, cock-tails. Jackie's listened in on the
extension. She's heard the man's voice.

Mr Black sells pharmaceuticals and has a station wagon
full of little samples that are uncounted. In Jackie's room we
listen to Meat Loaf and pop two tablets each of a happy pill
called *Probene, for the relief of stress, anxiety and mental
agitation.* 'Some relief,' Jackie snorts. 'It makes my head
itch.' As she rubs her scalp, a bright slit of genital pink shows
through the blond covering of hair. I ask if she thinks her dad
knows about her mom yet. 'You just asked me that,' she
snaps. I didn't just ask, I say, that was last week. 'Well not
much happens in a week.' But doesn't she think he wonders, I
want to know. Jackie rolls her eyes. 'He's an idiot.'

Images ping inside my head whenever I see Mrs Black.
Negligees. Gymnastic fucking. Fingernails shiny red.
Champagne room service in a suite overlooking the Eiffel
Tower. Jackie says she hasn't seen her parents kiss or hug
since she was a kid, and I imagine Mrs Black madly, tearfully
embracing a tall, trench-coated stranger. I expect her to be
transformed, but she still opens the door expressionlessly,
bulgy and baggy-eyed in her frayed terry-cloth robe, and she
still sighs when she sees it's me. With my parents Mrs Black is
all phony smiles, the good neighbour. But I get the sighs, and
she doesn't even bother to answer when I ask if Jackie's home,
just leaves me to watch her bum jiggle down the hall. Just a
kid, she thinks. Niceness not required. They're all different

............................................................................

when other adults aren't around. Maybe I shouldn't be so surprised that Mrs Black can turn into something else when she leaves in her car.

Waiting on my driveway for Jackie to return from piano isn't the most brilliant thing to be doing on a deep-freeze February morning. Especially when you're skinny, twiggy, leggy, a meatless bag of bones. In minutes my nostrils fill with snot crystals. My bangs cling to my frosty lashes and my bra hook pricks like a cold pin. I do a shuffling dance, wiggle my legs. Numbness begins pushing up from my fingers and toes like an anti-bloodstream, getting stronger the stiller I stand, the longer nothing happens.

The salt'n'sand plough finally made it out here to do the crescents in the night, make the snowbanks grow. Its scraping must have woken me. I remember opening my bedroom door and then this sudden undersea cavern, the hallway bathed in tropical blue. From the bathroom window I watched the truck flash down the street. It had thick wedged tires but seemed to be sailing away, a spray of broken ice and snow arcing from its plough.

Weekend days are long now. They were long before, but in the best way. I'd be tunnelling in that snow mound all afternoon, toasty in my snow pants and toque. God, snow pants! You couldn't pay me.

My boots make tight crunching sounds on the snow. The cold grazes my ears like a blade. A motor hums closer, closer, then the car, nothing like the Blacks', passes our street. What am I doing out here? Our lifeless block could be a scene from *The Omega Man* – would be, if you snuffed the heat jets rising from roof pipes, though even these don't prove that people are still alive inside. Traffic lights, thermostats – these things would go on by themselves for a while. Wheels rolling to stillness, the shake of a cut engine. I'm too poor to go downtown, too young to drive and too old for Saturday morning cartoons and snow forts. I've read about ancient Rome, the plantations and the pyramids, and those slaves had it bad, but I'm not complaining about bad, like my parents think, I'm talking about BORED. My brother yells that he can't listen to Jimi Hendrix first thing in the morning. It's his stereo, anyway. I come outside to freeze my buns.

Mr MacIntyre across the street gives me suspicious looks. Twice his spider-veined schnoz pokes through the sheers, and then he emerges to shovel the snow-throw at the end of his driveway. Tight jeans and make-up are his problem, I guess. Must keep an eye on the hooligans. Mr MacIntyre thinks he knows everything because he's older and owns a house, but like my parents, he just thinks he knows things. He'll see Mrs Black putting by in her car and think, 'Right-o, Mrs Black, going shopping, everything's normal, everything's good.' Frowns at me standing on my driveway (doing nothing), but has a smile for Becky Matthews here, who's delivering the paper. Thinks 'Becky Matthews, lovely-blond-red-cheeked-girl, hardworking, parents teach at the university.' My dad will shake his head in awe as Becky disappears across our yard: 'Look at that girl, plunging through the snow!' Responsible? Like shit – Becky's just greedy. Mr MacIntyre and Dad don't know that I'd do the paper route in a second except Becky's hogged it, inherited it from her brother and won't pass it on despite the fact that she's also grabbed the two best babysitting jobs on the block *and* apparently gets an unbelievable ten dollars a week allowance. Screw Becky Matthews.

..............................................................................................

Becky Matthews and her friends like volleyball, AM radio, horses, ponytails and braids, winning teams, other cute and popular girls, twenty-four-karat gold jewellery, frosted pink lip gloss, birthstone rings. In public school, Becky purposely crushed my toes on the court and hissed that I was *useless*, I was *making the team lose*. Becky and her friends don't stand on their driveways in midwinter when the street's so silent after Mr MacIntyre's shovelling, stand dreaming of being the Omega Man, the last one left alive. Wondering why it is that monsters always live alone.

I wince whenever I see Jackie's face at the door in the morning. She's behind all of us: tiny, boobless and buttless in her Vanderbilt jeans and still no period, so she tries to make-up for it by using way too much make-up, ha ha. Her rouge glows like distant stop lights through the icy pane (Stop in the name of love!). When she touches her nose to the glass she leaves a powdery beige print. If our situation were reversed, I know Jackie would be merciless. She can be meaner than anyone I've ever met, ten years of meanness walking to and from school together and over at each other's places, meanness always lurking, waiting to make a kill. But I can't do it back. I never could. Still, maybe I'm bad in a different way, for watching Jackie take her clown face to school. Maybe I'm even worse.

Lying on her bed, Jackie tosses me a copy of Jim Morrison's biography *No One Here Gets Out Alive* and tells me about the graffiti on his Paris grave. We talk about dead rock stars, John Bonham's recent 'drowning'. We decide to build a rock'n'roll catacomb in her room. It takes us all afternoon just to get the structure up, and then Jackie sulks and eats an entire bag of potato chips without offering me

........................................................

some when I tell her I can't stay for the evening. In public school, she would have planned some terrible revenge – stolen my diary and passed it around the school yard, started a rumour that I feasted on boogers – but she's got to watch it, got to be nicer now. She knows I'm going out to get high with Bono and that it's up to me to invite her because Bono's my friend. Jackie doesn't really have any other friends.

Cutting across the yard to my place, cursing at the snow wedging into my boots, I glance back at her pale window and imagine her watching as the Saturday night sky begins to twinkle with all the things she isn't doing. I also remember her tricks and taunts, the horrible, humiliating things she'd do to me with glee, things I thought would ruin my life forever – and I keep walking. Why should I show any mercy? Give me one good fucking reason.

Jackie's bedroom door now opens into a narrow tunnel. Stacked milk crates, leather-bound *Reader's Digest* volumes and laundry pins hold up musty-blanket walls. Daylight seeps through the wool. The fuzzy walls trap heat, make the passageway feel more like the inside of a mouth, or an intestine. 'Cool!' I laugh. Jackie cranks the music, Morrison's spooky 'The End'. We've built the tombs to sit against the catacomb walls like little altars. First stop is Jimi Hendrix: a glossy shot from a magazine safety-pinned to the wall, while underneath, a cardboard box draped with a sheet holds a black-baby doll that used to be Jackie's sister's, its body mummified in gauze bandages with a slit at the eyes. Across the mouth, red felt-pen letters spell OD'd. Tombs for Janis Joplin and Brian Jones come next, each illuminated with patio lanterns. A Jim Morrison poster with white paper x's taped to the pupils hangs above a shoebox grave with real potting soil

mounded inside. The Blacks' gold Christmas tree cross juts
from the dirt. We make John Bonham's grave last: a circle of empty
liquor bottles labelled with Led Zeppelin photos, the booze
ring enclosing a plastic Hallowe'en skull crossed with
drumsticks courtesy of Jackie's brother. Jackie and I haul her
stereo inside the tomb. We sit on the carpet and blast
'Welcome to My Nightmare', 'The Needle and the Damage
Done', 'Sister Morphine' and 'Hell's Bells', speculating on who
will be next.

Mr Black works late. Mrs Black goes out several times a week.
One evening when Mr Black comes home, he sits drinking the
guest Scotch in the kitchen, then walks into the TV room
where all the kids are sitting and says 'Where's your mother?'
Says it loud, and normally he's a quiet, mumbling sort of
man. 'Out,' Jackie tells him. Jackie and her sister know. Their
brother knows. 'Out where?' Mr Black demands, glaring at
them. Jackie shouts 'How the hell should *we* know?' and Mr
Black orders her to her room for being rude. When she
reaches the landing she yells 'You should take some bloody
Probene!'

Mrs Black's having an affair and driving around in her car,
still hosting the Greenview ladies' bridge club in her living
room, but my mom has a bird when she overhears me saying
*fuck* on the phone. You can do it but can't say it, right? But I
did the arithmetic, I know my brother was born six months
after the wedding. At the supper table I feel the world
separating, fissuring into pieces like those subterranean
plates. My parents care about speaking nicely and they
pretend things. There are gaps in their words, mystery spaces.

# Monsters

......................................................................

The bottle of pills on the bedside table, the phone number
stuck in the daybook, the dirty glass forgotten by the garage –
who knows what's connected to what. 'Fuck fuck fuck!' I say
to the street, standing on the driveway after dark. Wanting
the plough to skim by and take me into its aura of blue. Bury
them, or maybe me. Something.

Jackie takes her mother's Doulton figurines from the living-
room cabinet and lines them up inside the catacomb. In the
bonnet and parasol ladies' hands we place packets of Probene
and fake joints. We buy bags of Gold Rush nugget gum for
the little sacks and pull them empty over the ladies' heads.
Jackie insists that her mom won't notice because the living
room only gets used for company, but just when we've
finished illuminating our bag-faced chorus line with red
Christmas lights there's a loud thud and suddenly Mrs Black's
ducking inside the tunnel. Patio-lantern shadows under
bulging eyes and her mouth gaping, gasping as she takes
everything in. Hot shame rushes through me even though I
don't want it to, don't believe in it, and then Mrs Black draws
herself up and *my* jaw drops because there it is: a big, fresh
hickey on her throat. Her silky blouse and nice-lady slacks
(this is the clothing of an affair?), her white plastic beads,
and this welt like a tropical flower. Luscious red, bleeding to
purple at the centre. An eruption, a piece that doesn't fit,
doesn't fit at all and yet it does – I'm giggling now, this feeling
of wildness surging inside. The world's in pieces, a
kaleidoscope turning twenty-four hours a day with everyone
trying to make it stand still, freeze the picture, but they can't.
Mrs Black starting to scream at us can't. There's too many
pieces.

'Hideous!' Mrs Black shouts. I can't stop laughing.

## Stories

The first thing Regina ever said to me was 'Oh, you want to come over too? Okay, but you gotta please Willy.'

Grade eight. Kids were pouring out of the school bus around us. A small circle waited nearby, the girls already invited to come swimming at Regina's. I'd shared a seat with one of them on the way back from our Lambton Bog field trip. I was wearing my new Levi's, I'd gotten mud on them to make them look less new, and I'd acted cool enough that the girl had asked Regina if it was okay for me to come over too.

I said, 'Who's Willy?'

Regina squinted into the sun. Her chubby, freckled cheeks looked very white in the glare, very pure, and she smiled the way she usually does: like she knows all the things about you that you try to hide. She said, 'Willy's a retard who can't get any action, so we gals please him. You can't come over unless you do something to please him.'

'Like what?'

She screwed up her mouth. 'Oh, dance naked in the back yard, whatever. He'd like that.' She grinned again, the slight chip in her front tooth only noticeable because the others were perfect, and I remember thinking the word *sexy*. She's not pretty, but she's sexy. Plump and squeezable, already with an hour-glass figure and that knocked tooth. Her after-school parties were big gossip throughout grade eight. *Gerry Gordon and Paul Little come over and spin the bottle. She's been smoking since grade six. She lets Gerry feel her up. Her parents buy her booze.* Wild, the other kids called her. But the kids at our school were a bunch of stuck-up wussies. To me, kissing and drinking sounded close to paradise: London, Rome, the Riviera – where beautiful couples drink cocktails, and kiss.

I glanced at the other girls waiting and couldn't picture any of them twirling in the nude for a drooling moron. Of course Regina probably hadn't asked them to – they were her friends. It was just me, Miss Desperate.

'I'll moon him,' I blurted.

'Yow!' Regina waved the other girls over. 'Hey, Germaine here's gonna come and flash Willy!' The girls grinned and said 'cool', but they gave Regina secret looks that made me remember all the times I'd done dares before, and how people didn't like you more afterwards, they just thought you were stupid.

I went over to her house completely freaked because I didn't know if I could or should do what I'd promised, and what if I picked wrong and this was my only chance to get in with Regina forever? But it turned out that Willy, an older boy who goes to a special school and lives in the house behind Regina's, wasn't at home making woofing noises out his basement bedroom window at the girls swimming across the way, so I didn't have to do anything. But I was so happy to be there – the radio playing, Regina in her bikini and shades with her breasts jiggling as she sipped lemonade spiked with Scotch – that I did anyway, I pranced to the end of the deck and mooned Willy's window. And the girls shrieked because they were really too wimpy to do anything like it and because

there was a man mowing his lawn a few yards down who
might have seen, and Regina told the story during recess the
next day – except she made it longer and funnier, made it into
an actual dance that the man had seen, had bolted into his
house with a big woody denting his shorts – and everyone
screamed with laughter and I said I'd do it anytime, bring on
the Willys! And we all laughed more and Regina gave me a
secret look and afterwards invited me over again, just me,
and that was the start of it.

It's Monday at lunch almost a year later, and we're listening
to Regina talk about the weekend. She talks loud, partly
because the cafeteria's so noisy with hundreds of other
students and the ladies in uniforms clacking plates onto metal
trolleys. But Regina also likes to be loud, especially when
she's talking about sex or booze or dope, and when there's a
nearby table of ponytailed, music-geek girls to mortify.
Regina's already told us some juicy bits about her and Rick,
the music girls are deciding with puckered faces whether or
not to move to another table, and Regina's coming to later in
the evening, the part where I topple a Morgen tombstone with
a Scotch and Coke in my hand.

'She scared the shit out of us! Me and Rick are walking in
the dark, and all we see is this bony white hand rising from
the ground behind the stone, holding up a plastic cup.'
Regina picks up a pop can and raises it trembling above the
table.

'At least I didn't spill it,' I say.

'And then she starts groaning.' Still holding up the can,
Regina rolls her eyes and contorts her face in death throes.
'Ack! Oh! Uuugh!' Everyone's laughing, another Germaine-
as-a-spaz story.

..........................................................................

'Hey!' I try to defend myself. 'That stone fucking hurt.'

'The Morgens! You *idiot*.' This is Jackie, who hasn't missed a chance to remind me I'm idiotic since kindergarten – especially in front of anyone else I become friends with. At the word Morgens the music-geek girls stop folding up their wax paper lunches to listen. 'You're cursed, you know,' Jackie goes on. 'You're totally fucked.' Everyone around our table's nodding, serious expressions on their faces.

I roll my eyes like this is nonsense. 'It was an *accident*. Don't you know how dark graveyards are at night?'

Jackie shakes her head. Her eyes sparkle, she looks so pleased she could hug herself. She points a skinny finger at my chest. 'Spirits don't care about accidents. You are definitely and eternally FUCKED.'

The Morgen family are sort of famous around here for being involved in a child murder a hundred-odd years ago. At least the townspeople up in Lodell believed the Morgens were, so they torched their farmhouse, killing some of the family inside. People say the whole thing happened because the Morgens were really Jews or Gypsies or something, even devil worshippers, though they denied it. They're all buried in the graveyard outside Lodell. Every Hallowe'en the paper reports how someone has graffitied the tombstones with swastikas or pentangles again.

I can't tell whether Jackie's serious and I'm not sure I believe in curses anyway. Still, does believing really matter, if you've been targeted? 'Well I seem to be okay so far,' I shrug. 'Except for my leg.'

'Let's see!' says Bono, who loves injuries and scars, and I'm glad to change the subject. She comes around and squats among the chair legs beside me. Dangling my leg, I hike my jeans, but they're too tight to reveal more than the bottom few inches of the purplish welt that streaks right up to my hip. I remember whacking into the edge of the tombstone and grinding face-first into the ground, a mouthful of grass, the stone breezing my hair as it wumped beside my head.

Bono pushes up her glasses, peers carefully and whistles, obviously impressed. This is good, since she's the toughest of us all. Then she presses her thumb into the dark spot of the bruise and grins. 'That hurt?'

Regina still has lots to tell. For the rest of lunch she talks about the dope Nark and Rick brought, Nark's crazy driving, and fooling around with Rick. She exaggerates everything ('He drove, like, 150 down this gravel road! Me and Germ were practically puking in the back'). She seems to have forgotten I was there, or decided it doesn't matter. I watch Jackie and Bono. Don't they realize? Why don't they question and sneer, as they would to me? My leg throbs where Bono pressed it. Regina has this ability with stories: her bounciness and giggle, that smile. Like hypnotism.... Still, as the story winds down I start to get worried. Rick all over her ... dancing in the road.... Regina isn't just exaggerating, she's *twisting*. Telling it wrong, all wrong. When she pauses to take a sip of pop, I butt in.

'Yeah,' I say, 'and then those assholes took off!'

Regina looks at me. Jackie and Bono lift their chins, like they've caught a scent.

'They took off?' Jackie asks.

'Only for a little while Germ,' Regina says in a chiding voice, as if I'm the one who's wildly exaggerating. 'They were just being drunk idiots.' Then she plunges on, telling us about her and Rick making out on what they thought was the grass, rolling over and realizing it was one of those poor-person graves that's marked only with a small stone laid into the earth. Everyone agrees that that's nothing compared with knocking over a Morgen tombstone. Obviously this is the detail that's stuck, that everyone will razz me about for days, maybe weeks.

When the first bell rings I stay behind. I join the growing line-up to buy some lemonade before the cafeteria closes. As I wait I can see Regina and the others through the window, gathered outside under the smoking pit's roof. Some guy friends of ours have joined them, but there's no sign of Rick and Nark. I wonder if we'll ever talk to them again.

Other people in the cafeteria are also watching Regina. New school, new students, and already she's the centre of gossip. Near the window, a table of asshole preppie boys are snickering. One nods toward Regina and jams his tongue into his cheek: *Blow Job Queen*. Of course they're all dying for blow jobs they've never had and I want to smack the grins off their faces. But even though the nickname's ridiculous – she's never even done it – if Regina had seen, she probably would have just laughed and said 'That's right. And which one of you boys is the King?'

The line shuffles forward. A fiery pain darts up my leg. Worsening, it seems. I press my palm to my forehead, which feels swollen, weighted.

In the chaos before last bell I hobble up the seething stairs to class, find my desk. While the teacher monotones I stare out the window at the rooftops of our neighbourhood, a black wave rolling toward the trees by the river. I drink the lemonade. I'm trying to compress those last cold hours of Friday night into some place small and unnoticeable – into a few minutes that can be waved aside without blinking. Maybe that's really where they belong? But they won't fit. They keep popping out again, the memories taking over my head until

...........................................................

they're so heavy I seem immobilized, aching all over like I've been crushed by that fallen stone.

I could see Regina's bent head through the bodies pushing down the hallway after last bell on Friday afternoon. She stood up with our fat *Biology Nine* text wedged in her armpit and a red pencil case between her teeth.

'Uh!' she said through the plastic.

'Reg!'

She grabbed a binder from the top shelf and slapped this up against the textbook without taking her eyes from me.

'Uhuh-uhh?'

I put my hand on the pencil case and pulled it out, along with a long silvery line of drool that snapped and landed on my leg.

'How's it goin'?' she grinned.

'Wet.'

'You want wet? Check this out.' She nodded at the locker and parted the two jean jackets hanging inside. 'Come into the House of the Holy,' she whispered. Taped to the locker's back wall was a centrefold from *Playgirl* of a guy with a massive hard-on, floating on his back in a pool. His dick was like something pulled from inside his gut: deep red against the tanned stomach, the turquoise pool liner. A cut-out picture of Robert Plant's face – contorted in mid-'Stairway to Heaven' screech – had been stuck over the model's.

'Jesus,' I gasped.

'No,' Regina said, with a teacherly frown, 'it's *Lord Robert.*'

'Oh. Dear Robert.'

'Who art in England.' Regina bowed her head.

'Hallowed be thy hair.'

......................................................................

'Thy cockdom come.'

'Thy lust be done.'

'On my willing body.'

'As it is on mine.' We nodded solemnly. Regina let the jackets fall in place and we turned and caught an autobody geek from our grade gawking.

'Learn something new?' she demanded.

Geekboy grimaced and edged away down the hall. 'You're crazy,' he muttered, looking us up and down like we were mutants. 'Totally fuckin' crazy.'

'Yeah,' Regina said, beaming. 'Praise the Lord.'

'So what's the plan?'

'The plan is for you to entertain us for the evening using only your body and a beer bottle.'

I arched one eyebrow, a look I've been getting really good at, and said 'Oh please.'

Regina made a face like that famous scream painting as she put on mascara. I rolled over on the matted shag carpet and opened the jacket to *Dark Side of the Moon*, thinking I could lie forever in Regina's room, propped on tasselled pillows from India and surrounded by pictures of Led Zeppelin and Jim Morrison, by incense and gauzy scarves and coloured light bulbs lighting up fantastic velvet posters so they glow against the dark walls like windows onto phosphorescent worlds. All the changes I've made to my bedroom are cheap imitations of hers. Sometimes I think that's all I'll ever be. Regina, Jackie, Bono – they're all different, themselves. I just react.

'So what *is* the plan?' I asked again, scanning the lyrics for the billionth time.

'Meet Rick and Nark at seven-thirty.'

..................................................................

'Who's Nark?'

Regina churned the bristled handle in the tube. 'Fucking hell, I'm almost out.' She leaned into the dresser mirror again and her cleavage became a deep rift. Regina's always joking about her tits, as she calls them. Sometimes it's priceless, like at a party when she'll strut past some ogling guy and say 'Do that much longer and your face will freeze, you know.'

In the distance a door banged, heels clomped across the kitchen floor. I reached to flick the volume down and heard Regina's mom yelling *'appreciate it!'*

'Hello Deirdre!' Regina called in a chirrupy voice.

'Who's Nark?'

'Friend of Rick's. *Cute.*' She tossed the mascara and lip gloss onto my lap and gave me her fluttery eyelids look.

'What did you tell him about me?'

'Nothing!' She began to fluff and scrunch her hair, misting the curls with spray. 'Jeez Germ, you're such a worrier.'

'Okay, okay,' I snapped. She knows I hate being called that – it makes me sound like my parents. Yet I've seen Regina setting people up, convincing them with lines like 'He creams himself whenever he sees you, you know,' or 'She totally wants your ass – she's just shy,' and I would die if someone said that about me. But Regina believes it's better this way, else people are too cowardly and no one would ever have any fun. Considering I wouldn't meet guys otherwise, I guess this is kind of true. And I can't forget those days before I knew her: the humiliation of snowball dances, oblivious boys sauntering past, scouting the faraway land of pretty girls. Now they come around, and Regina's the one who can do the talking. I owe everything to her, and she knows it.

'Look! There they are.'

Pulled up behind the school's smoking pit was an orange
Pinto that flashed pink in the setting sun. The guys were
leaning against the hood. They're two grades ahead of us, but
I already knew Rick from a party Regina and I went to
recently. By the end of the night the two of them had been out
in the backyard, caught mashed together on a deck chair
when the cops came and kicked everyone out.

'Hiya!' Regina called.

'Hey.' Rick's eyes flicked over her body. He did the same to
me, as did his friend, Nark. Unlike Rick, who looked a bit
angelic, like a young Roger Daltrey, Nark was not cute.
Under stringy hair he had a pasty, sunken-looking face like a
large saucer and his slouchy, bow-legged body was wrapped
in skin-tight clothes, even his jean jacket. He held a cigarette
tight between his lips, and something about his mouth hinted
that his teeth tilted inward. I said hi, avoiding eye contact.
I'm finding that I have to do this with certain boys or else
they automatically get the wrong idea, and something about
the nervous way Nark jammed his fists in his pockets and
kicked at a cigarette butt on the cement make me think he
was one of these.

Regina stood very close to Rick, waiting for him to touch
her. She was smiling her other smile, the one she doesn't use
very often. Sometimes I think it's her real smile, sweet and
very soft, like her cheeks. But that's not true. They're all real.

Rick grinned, but his hands stayed at his sides. Finally
Regina switched smiles and pointed at me.

'Nark, this is my friend Germaine-German-Germ,
daughter of Krauts. Her parents were Nazis.'

'Nazis, eh?' Nark said, and smiled. I saw I was right about
the teeth.

'Oh yeah, big time.' I grinned at Regina, both of us

........................................................

picturing my parents, flat-assed in their armchairs in front of
*Masterpiece Theatre* with Kleenexes balled into their cardigan
sleeves.

'Let's hit it,' Rick said, and they opened the car door.
Regina and I squeezed in behind the bucket seats. I moved
my feet around, trying to create some room in the tangle of
jumper cables and garbage. Nark lit another smoke, wedged
it in the corner of his mouth, and eyed me in the rear-view.

'You comfortable back there?'

'I'm fine.'

His cigarette flared. Smoke rose from the tip in a bluish
line, hit the roof and spread into a haze that blurred Nark's
eyes. He seemed to be waiting. 'It's fine, thanks,' I said again,
and smiled. This seemed to satisfy him and he leaned to start
the engine. Regina jabbed my leg with her knuckle and I
jabbed her back.

'Okay, let's blow this scene!' Nark said as he threw the car
into gear and we shot through the school gates. He whacked
Rick's shoulder. 'Music!' A cassette clicked into place and the
speakers crackled painfully with static. 'An old record. Sorry
'bout that,' Nark said, singling me out in the mirror again.

'Very HB,' Regina whispered. I glared at her to shut up.

'What's that?' Rick's grinning face appeared between the
seats and Regina goosed his nose, but then the opening of
'More Than a Feeling' started up and seconds later we
couldn't hear anything else. We were speed-weaving through
crescents in the north end of the neighbourhood, passing the
occasional frowning adult getting into a car, or group of kids
on bikes who stared. We were approaching Arbor Lake Road,
and as Nark cut another corner and Regina and I tipped back
and forth on the seat and I caught a glimpse of the
speedometer reading something I really didn't want to know, I

thought about HB, huge balls, and wondered if Regina had
drunkenly told Rick the other ones: HC and NA. It's her code.
('Germ, check it out – three o'clock. Holy HC!') Regina's
more of an expert on this stuff because she's given a hand job,
while I've never even touched a C. Hand jobs, blow jobs,
finger fucks – there's so much else to *do* now. Here I was
panicked about my first kiss only a year ago.

I watched Nark's fingers tap his cigarette. I doubted he had
either an HC or HB – not that I wanted to know. He looked
too hollowed out, like there was nothing left beneath his skin
but ash.

Nark drove north. We climbed out of the valley, passed the
Wellington city limits sign (Regina's announcement: 'City
Dimwits: 200,000') and hit highway speed. After about ten
minutes we reached Lodell and Nark swerved onto a
concession road. Despite the gravel he didn't slow down. He
was smoking another cigarette, and with the windows barely
cracked the air inside the car was as dense as the dust cloud
churned up by the wheels. Suddenly he braked and pulled
over. We got out in front of the Lodell cemetery. The old
church was boarded up and the gates locked, but we easily
jumped the peeling iron fence.

On the other side, I felt like we'd entered a different
element, like dropping into a pool. I hung back and watched
the others wind through the tombstones. The cemetery isn't
large, but it's big enough to roam around in. Unclipped weeds
and wildflowers had sprouted along its perimeters, and
beyond, I could see the hard furrowed soil of a farmer's field. I
strolled among the stones, most of them eroded, illegible. All
around was a heavy, pressing quiet – the way an empty
church feels, though the fence could hardly do that. A strange
heaviness, because it felt like it was lifting me up at the same

................................................................

time. I breathed in the smell of spring grass. I opened my
arms to the breeze.

I found the others standing around a tall monument.
Already the guys' jean jackets were blending into the blue
twilight. Lights in Lodell hung pale in the east. Regina
handed me my drink and Rick passed around a spliff. I'd
noticed earlier the gold hawk-ornament chain he was wearing
and asked where he got it. Nark laughed for the first time
and said it was a love token from Rick's old squeeze, Chrissie
Patchett.

I looked at Regina. Nark *must* be joking. Chrissie
Patchett? A scary-looking wrestler of a girl who's supposedly
the biggest slut at our school. I didn't think anyone actually
dated her. Juicy Snatchett, she's called.

'Fuck you,' Rick said to Nark, but he was grinning
proudly. 'It's cool.'

'It is,' Regina said, and went to peer at the necklace more
closely. She fingered it for a moment, then Rick put his hand
on her hip and pulled her into his chest. They kissed. I
pictured Rick doing this with Chrissie Patchett and felt
revolted. Then, thinking about the gift of the necklace, sad.

When we'd finished the next spliff it was completely dark,
no stars or moon. Rick and Regina slipped away, leaving
Nark and me the rest of the Scotch. I listened to Regina's
fading giggle and swore to myself.

Using his lighter to see, Nark was squatting to mix another
set of drinks in the big plastic cups. Wonderful. We had, so
far, said nothing to each other since the car. I vowed never to
go on another double date. I thought about following Regina
('Let's go see what those guys are doing!'). I considered
suggesting we build a fire – it would at least give us
something to do. Nark handed me my drink. 'Another one

for the lady,' he said, then leaned against the monument
beside me, a dark and spidery shape whose jacket touched
mine.

We looked at the distant lights.

I said, 'So, uh, what does Nark stand for anyway?' My
voice came out as a mumble, muffled by the night and that
eerie graveyard stillness like listening ears.

'You don't know about Nark?' He turned, and I made out
the outline of his head, a whitish blur that could have been
his smile. 'Shit, that's a pretty dangerous thing not to know,'
he said. His body shifted and I heard him rummaging in his
pockets. 'The Narkster's the one who's gonna get you for
having *this*,' he whispered, and sparked the lighter. In his
palm was a tiny plastic vial of hash oil with a bright red cap.

'Oh right,' I smiled. Nark equals narcotics officer.
Plainclothes undercover agents who people say infiltrate all
the high schools, posing as students.

'Rick came up with it,' Nark explained, putting the lighter
away and repositioning his arm more firmly against mine. 'I
started dealing in grade eight.'

'Wow.' I wondered if he'd had better posture back then,
before the limp hair, the bruised-looking crescents under his
eyes.

Nark lit a cigarette. He managed to do this using one arm,
so that the band of warmth where our bodies met remained
unbroken. I wanted to run right then, but it's not easy, saying
no. Nark's fingers brushed my thigh, then settled there. I had
to move. Yet part of me was stuck. When someone wants
something so badly from you, something so normal,
something that can be so easy, is it really right not to let them
have it? Especially when everyone else says no?

The fingers pressed against my leg. I had to move now.

..........................................................................

'This stone's getting cold,' I said. I stepped away from the monument and noticed my head seemed to lag behind. The drink I was sipping left a burning film in my throat. The ground tilted slightly, righted itself again, and I imagined the bodies below rolling over, like disturbed sleepers.

I listened for Regina and Rick. The only noise was a breeze rustling the grass, and an airy echo that could have been cars on the highway or wind travelling high above our heads. Nark touched my elbow and I spun around.

'Shotgun?' he asked. The voice was disembodied, only connected to the invisible mouth by a glowing spliff, which as I watched rotated in the air and vanished. I felt something warm on my face, and Nark put a hand on my shoulder and drew me forward until our bangs almost touched. I opened my mouth as little as possible to inhale the smoke. Nark's fingers slid across my shoulder. He couldn't very well kiss me with a spliff in his mouth, but what about after? We seemed to be heading down some unalterable road – or Nark was, steering pedal to the metal now, and the higher that speedometer rose the tougher it was to break away, bail out. As soon as he took that spliff out of his mouth –

'Whoah!' I gasped, staggering away. The bright cinder reappeared in the dark and started to come closer.

'You okay?'

'Fine!' I coughed and put up my hand. 'I just have to pee like crazy.' Then I backed off, ducked behind a tombstone, and started to run.

Regina and Rick found me on the ground.

'Are you okay? What the fuck are you doing? Where's Nark?' She and Rick held their lighters over my face. I moaned and giggled, dizzy, half-conked with pain, but happy to be reunited with them. Rick looked around and shouted 'Hey Nark! Whoo-hoo! Studly!' There was no answer. He said he'd be back in a minute.

'What happened with Nark?' Regina asked.

'He's being a slime. I came to find you.'

'You don't like him?'

'No.'

'Oh. Shit.' She sounded a bit nervous, and I wondered again what she'd said to set the night up. She sat down on the edge of the fallen tombstone and flicked her lighter. 'Hey! You downed a Morgen.'

'Great. Call the newspaper.'

Regina chuckled. 'So, what did Nark do?'

I told her the details.

'Oh, with this shotgun I thee wed,' she said.

'Oh baby, kiss me with your spliff.'

'Oh yes!' Regina groaned and lay back on the tombstone, writhing. 'Oh Nark darlin', run your hot, flaming cylinder over my body. Let me go down on my knees and whiff your sweet-smellin' spliff!'

We busted up laughing and I yowled because my leg hurt like hell and we laughed some more. 'And did you do any whiffing with Rick?' I asked, scooting my fingers across her chest, and she yelped that *maybe* she had, just maybe, then bolted upright.

'What was that?'

It was too dark to see anything, but I realized that the concession must be close. A car engine was turning over almost beside us. In a minute came the opening bars of 'More Than a Feeling.'

'Let's go.' Regina got up clumsily, lurched, said 'whoops!' just like her mother and started off. I limped toward the

music. As I was straining over the fence, the Pinto's
headlights snapped on. Regina was lit up on the road. She
waved to the guys invisible in the car, then started to dance.
The Pinto crunched toward her, its beams like two probing
limbs. Suddenly the car accelerated and spun around. It sat
idling, and as Regina and I walked toward it my head went
very clear. I remembered something from a long time ago,
except I was walking toward a bicycle then. I'd been double
riding with Jackie, maybe arguing or maybe not, and she was
waiting for me, straddling her bike, and when I was almost
there –

The Pinto took off.

A voice, I think Rick's, cackled into the dark: *See you,
you –!* But the name he called us got drowned in gravel, and I
was glad.

At first, Regina believed they'd be right back. I wasn't so sure.
We watched the tail lights recede down the road, rise up a
hill, and vanish. We waited. We shared a smoke. Then
without talking about it, we started toward the highway. By
the time we climbed that hill the road ahead was black.
Regina swore. She yelled RICK MACLEAN IS A PUNY DICK
CHILD MOLESTER, and other things, to the roadside trees.

We picked up our pace.

I tried not to notice the throb in my leg and wished it were
later in the year, a humid July night instead of early May with
a northern wind shivering across the fields. I thought about
my parents waiting up for me and how many weeks'
grounding I'd get when I got home. And what kind of
explanation I could give. And where to buy some gum to
cover up my Scotch breath.

I wondered if this ever happened to Chrissie Patchett.

In silence, we reached the empty highway. Under the whine of electric street lights we headed up the deserted street, past the darkened gas station, another church, the farm supply and convenience stores in Lodell. A block of serene Victorian houses, then the old grey mill that still makes flour. 'That's a cool building,' I said, then regretted this lame attempt to be cheery. Regina sniffed and wiped her nose on her jacket. Her check gleamed wet.

The town dwindled at our backs as we trudged along the gravel shoulder. I knew it would take a very, very long time to get home. Whenever headlights approached, creeping slowly down the long straight road and exposing us on that empty plain as the wheels slowed or sped by indifferent, I thought about hitchhiking and all the terrible stories you hear about people getting killed or disappearing. And even when, after another hour or so, the Pinto returned and drove us home, Regina and I both ignoring Rick's goofy 'It was just a joke' excuses, I still thought about what would have happened if we'd never come back. The school cafeteria, everyone with a theory. Rumours, gossip – the crazy stories that people would believe. Months and years passing and no one would ever know what actually happened, who we really were. This seemed to be the worst thing of all, the doom that replayed in my head like a scratched record. However bad dying was, it would only happen once. But the lies, like restless ghosts, would go on forever.

After Monday's last class is over I go to Regina's locker to meet her. I still have my vice-grip headache. I stand against the cool metal with my eyes closed and feel the breeze from students rushing down the hallway to leave.

'Hey baby.' Regina wafts up smiling and pinches me on

the bum. She hands me her books while she spins the lock and that's when I am about to tell her that she shouldn't have cut me off at lunch, Rick and Nark are pigs and everyone should know it. But before I can say this she starts telling me about some event from the afternoon, and soon I'm laughing and I'm feeling better – because she really is funny, and as we leave I'm already shuffling the last few hours for a story that she'll like, ignoring the heaviness that's still there somewhere inside me, that I know isn't going away now. It really isn't, is it?

........................................................................

# A Short Chronicle
# of Tenth-Grade Love

**Debbie Deering**
Debbie Deering behind me in French has an engagement ring
on her finger. She's not the first in our grade. So do two other
girls, and I've heard there are more.

'It's freaky,' Debbie whispers one day (she hardly gets any
louder, except for little yelps or squeals), 'but I really feel
Tony's my destiny.'

'Destiny?' I shift sideways in my chair. We're supposed to
be working on the pronoun *celui*.

She nods quickly and I use the moment to eyeball the row
of hickeys on her neck, peeking out from under the pink
cowl-neck sweater. 'Like fate, you know?' she says, making
her adorable brown eyes bigger. Debbie's always been pretty.
She went to my public school, we had a lot of grades together
and she was a princess all those years too, always a teacher's
pet. Unlike most pretty girls though, Debbie's mostly friendly
and nice. For example, she talks to someone like me.

'I'm positive I dreamt about him before we met,' she's
saying. 'I just remembered it the other night, after he asked
me to marry him. I remembered I used to always dream about
this guy, and he was so similar, you know? I think it must
have been him.'

'Wow.' My dreams are all about weird houses and

............................................................

psychedelic landscapes and people doing awful things like they're normal.

'Yeah,' she sighs.

'So, the guy in the dream was your husband?'

She bites her bottom lip. 'I'm not sure. Hmm. I don't remember the dreams well. I mean, what actually happened in them. But the guy was definitely Tony. It's just so wild, isn't it?'

'Uh-huh.'

Tony: thick moustache and feathered hair, in grade thirteen but looks twenty-five, drives a Trans Am. Sexy and stupid-looking, like John Travolta. So where did he get the bucks for that rock? All I know about him is that he gets in lots of fights. Debbie once told me she cried when her brother skewered a caterpillar on a Popsicle stick. I wonder if she goes all the way with Tony.

Giggling so her black curls jiggle, Debbie puts her fists to her chest and squirms in her chair. She looks incredibly sweet as she does this.

I bite my thumbnail. 'So ... you're really getting married?' I can't believe I'm having this conversation in grade ten. *Married.*

'Yeah,' Debbie says with a sigh, and her minty sweet breath touches me. She shows me the ring again. It's a big one.


### Detention Room Girl

She has the smallest diamond I've ever seen.

'It's a diamond chip,' she explains, holding her hand over my desk and spreading long, manicured fingers that seem to belong to another person. 'For now, until we have the money for a better one later.'

I stare. Where the diamond's supposed to be are two tiny clasps, rising up from the band and joining – but there's nothing in between. Then she rotates her hand and I catch a gleam, like the hint of water through a sewer grate.

We figure out we've never met because she's in MacKenzie's four-year diploma program and I'm in the five, and the two have hardly any common classes. General Level Diploma, hers is called. I don't even know how I got in the Advanced, or how anyone got anywhere, except that almost all the General Level kids, like her, live across the river in Morwood Park, a neighbourhood of bungalows and townhouses. Still, you'd think we all would have been given the choice, at some point.

I ask her about her boyfriend, saying 'boyfriend' because I just can't say 'fiancé' like she does. He doesn't go to this school. He doesn't go to school at all, actually. He works two jobs, doing construction and in a restaurant kitchen. He's saving money. They've been seeing each other since she was thirteen and he was seventeen, and she's doing detention for skipping classes to go to his place (for sex, I bet). She tells me all about their plans without once smiling.

'Next year I'll be old enough to start working and he'll get me into the restaurant.'

'Holy shit,' I say, because the thought of a job makes me cringe. She looks at me funny. 'I mean that would be cool, working in a restaurant,' I nod. 'Probably lots of parties.' She agrees, not seeming very interested. She looks much older than fifteen: almost six feet tall and big. Not fat, really, just large: thick wrists at the top of those graceful hands, big mama boobs, a wide jaw – like one of those pioneer farm girls in old photos. Pregnant at seventeen, dead at twenty-five.

..................................................................

## Gavin

'What are you thinking, Germaine?'

This is what he keeps asking. It kind of freaks me out.

'Me? I have no thoughts. Mind vacant.'

'Got that right,' says Regina.

'Bullshit.' Gavin grins.

I start to laugh. Partly because I'm shitting it, because Gavin's come too close – flirting close – and all I can think about is jumping his bones. Dark eyes sparky and teasing, and now Regina's watching. As her best buddy, I'm supposed to be helping. I stop smiling.

Seems like every month Regina has a new guy to drool over, but Gavin's something else – she's crazy for him. What can I do? I guard how I look at him, especially since he keeps looking back. I've tried ignoring him but couldn't take it, it seemed cruel, and besides, I don't want him to think I'm a bitch. We're all supposed to be friends, or whatever. So I stare when neither he nor Regina will notice. Ration my peeks. Or I don't meet his eyes. At least, not for more than a second or two. And even that's too much.

He peers at me, an animal behind the soft black bars of his bangs. He has a small taut ass that I want to feel. His scent makes my throat hurt.

If he would just fall for Regina, everything would be easy.

My night dreams are of houses where there's no electricity. Normally I'm alone. I creep through the dark and peer into rooms where a man, chuckling, helps his wife hang up Christmas decorations and two nooses for them to die, where families eat supper while a bear munches something white and bloody in the dog bowl. Crazy shit. Lately, Gavin's been appearing. There's never sex. We're usually slinking about together, whispering close. Once we were eluding some bike gang that was going to kill us. Another time we were looking for a bedroom to rest in, but every room had something absurdly wrong with it, the floor caved in, beds suspended over pits. In that dream he reached back for my hand as we climbed the stairs and when I woke up there was a moment before I opened my eyes when I was still holding it. I can still recall the feeling of its weight.

During school I always end up fantasizing about us – even when I can't stand it any more, when my head hurts from wanting him so much, like when you go hungry too long. But the fantasies are like movies that just keep rolling, class after class. Gavin and I finding each other in the smoking rubble of MacKenzie after a nuclear strike. Gavin and I at Regina's funeral. Gavin being adopted by my parents. When I actually see him it's bizarre: you'd think a person would somehow know what trips you're doing with them in your mind. There should be a physcial law. Yet though Gavin's questions make me paranoid, he really knows nothing – except that Regina wants to gobble him alive.

In my favourite daydream we're in the ravine. It's fall, the leaves all shades of fire, the sun brilliant. Regina has fallen in love with someone else. Free, Gavin and I skid down the slope behind my old public school and head into the woods, me showing him the best spots. We romp around for hours and he loves it, gets right into skipping stones by the river, fossil hunting. Lastly, I lead him to the sand dunes, where kids ride their dirt bikes. They're not really dunes, just knobby hills grooved with trails and covered in tall grass. We find a patch to do what we really came here for, and sit down, hidden. The grass swishes and bends. Gavin takes my hands, which are

45

cold, and slides them under his jacket against his ribs. But I can't fill in the rest. I stop at his face, lips parted, coming closer. I can see the redness inside. His breath smells faintly of smoke.

### Too drunk, guy from another school

'You were so! You were behind the couch on the floor making out with him!'

'No way.'

'Ask Bono! She saw it too. We were howling.'

'You lie.'

'German!' Regina pushes me, laughing. 'Look at you! You shouldn't be so embarrassed. He wasn't *that* ugly.'

All I remember is a peach-fuzz moustache. I have this close-up, photographic image of it looming unsteadily above me. I can only see the moustache and the lips it's attached to, which are wet, open, and have pieces of dead skin scaling off them. The rest of the picture's murky, like the mouth's emerging from darkness. When I woke up the next day, after I'd puked my brains out, I thought I'd dreamt this. Maybe I did.

### Nick François, drunk

A bunch of us are at a big bash during Christmas holidays and I go upstairs to use the can. As I reach the top step, a door to one of the rooms flings open and this girl rushes out past me. The hallway light illuminates a figure inside: Nick, sitting on a bed.

'Hey, Nick?' I call. His pose makes me speak softly. Head bowed, shoulders limp. The bed still perfectly made.

Nick raises his head then drops it again. I've never seen him like this. Is he just really wasted? I come slowly closer, sit down on the end of the bed.

# A Short Chronicle of Tenth-Grade Love

............................................................................

'Nick, are you okay?'

'No.' Voice thick, but not just with booze. He's crying.

Nick François. Showed up at school in September and is already transferring out next term to Central Collegiate, which apparently is a billion times cooler than MacKenzie (what wouldn't be?), and is where he was supposed to go in the first place, except there was some registration mix-up. Nick's mother's an actress at Stratford and their downtown house is full of Persian carpets and African sculpture, groovy photographs of musicians and a vast record collection. But no one knew this when Nick arrived. All we knew was that he was so incredibly gorgeous and cool it was like he wasn't a real person. Best of all: he shunned the preppies.

He wasn't rude or anything – that's not his style. Regina and I scoped him in the cafeteria the first day at lunch. 'I bet you he's British,' Regina said. 'Or American.' While Nick was in the food line-up the preppie contingent sent one of their best bitches, Tracey Prince (rich and beautiful), to invite him to sit with them. No one else had asked, so he did. He ate lunch at the preppie table for a couple of weeks, and then one lunch period he didn't show up.

Regina and I watched the preppies looking about for him, glancing up whenever the cafeteria doors opened. Everyone was still trying to figure out what Nick François was. Even though he'd been sitting with the preppies he sure didn't seem like one, with his silk-lined, Mod-style leather coat – like something out of *Quadrophenia* – his sexy mellow voice and bum-swaying walk, and wavy hair going well below the preppies' standard collar line. And he seemed, well, too nice for them. Once as I tremblingly passed him in the hallway, he met my eyes with a smile I've never seen on a guy, which said he knew exactly what I was thinking and hey, that was cool.

We'd heard about his mother by then, and that he'd been born in France. People also said he smoked.

When it was clear Nick wasn't coming to the cafeteria, Regina and I headed out to the smoking pit, where everyone who isn't a preppie, geek, jock, Christian or keener hangs out. At MacKenzie, this leaves a pathetically small crowd, so we all know each other. We're hanging, chatting it up and having our smokes, when suddenly the metal doors clang open and out steps Nick François. Boom: the noise drops, domino-style, as people clue-in, until except for the seniors out in the parking lot by their cars, we're all talking in whispers, pretending conversation while staring. Every girl on the pit wanted Nick and every guy did too, in a different way.

Along the inside pit wall runs the cafeteria window. The preppies in our grade have always claimed the tables right next to it, so all through lunch period, day after day, they sit inside, watching us through the glass. Gossiping. Never coming out. Nick moved until he was right in front of this window with his back to it. Just stood there calmly, with the faces on either side gawking. Took out a pack of smokes: Marlboros. Sparked one with the flick of a silver lighter. Exhaled. Placed his eyes on the distance.

Hand it to Regina for making us not look like complete fools. She put on a big smile and strutted on over to introduce herself. Nick smiled back and shook her hand, so gracious. Jesus, it was like having Mick Jagger visit! We waited for Regina's next move. That's when the best part happened.

*The preppies came out to the pit.* Tracey Prince, Annabel Lucas, David Reitman, Jonathan Wellesley, Nichola LaFleche – the five of them so casual, like they owned the place: the guys with their hands in their cotton pants pockets, the girls all slinky smiles. We've lost already, I thought. Sporty turtlenecks and LaCoste shirts in the middle of denim-and-leather land. They swarmed Nick. Talk about desperate! They were actually trying to *retrieve* him. And Nick, brilliant, says to them, 'Oh hey, do you know my friend Regina?' Friend! The preppies think we're all a bunch of pothead losers and sluts. No status. Nick was tipping the scale our way.

'Come on,' I said to our group, and went over to join them. Introductions all around. Now we outnumbered the preppies, and they had nothing to do: they don't smoke, they don't buy drugs, they hate all of us. As we talked with Nick you could see them getting more anxious, unused to being second best to anything. They fell silent. Lost their we-belong-here grins. Then they left – fast. That was our first victory, probably the only one we'll ever get. I think we all held our breath until the doors had shut. Then Nick looks at us, smiling. 'Well! That sure was *tense*.' Brilliant. From then on, he hung out with us.

Nick François with tears running down his cheeks. He crosses his arms over his stomach and starts rocking, his breath in little gasps. No guy's ever cried in front of me. In fact, no one's ever cried in front of me like this: real crying, not the usual stuff, where your eyes get wet and you look away so your friends don't see. I'm not sure what I'm supposed to do. I'm afraid to touch him – that he'll think it's a desperate come-on or something, like taking advantage of a wounded exotic animal that would otherwise snarl or flee. On the other hand, I can't just sit here like I don't care.

Sliding closer on the bed, I reach out and lay my hand on Nick's forearm. I move my thumb across the soft, downy skin. *My God, I'm touching Nick François.* Likely the best-looking male flesh I'll ever have contact with.

..................................................................

Bent over like he has a bellyache, Nick doesn't move. 'Nick, what's wrong?' I ask. 'Who was that girl?'

'Her name's Sarah,' he croaks, voice all gooey.

'Who is she?'

'She used to be my girlfriend.' He lifts his arm to wipe his nose, even his snot clear and perfect and probably sweet, and I take my hand away. It was a signal, you see: he could have used the other hand. I fold my fingers in my lap.

'Used to be?'

'Before I came here. MacKenzie, I mean. We went out for a year. And then she dumped me.'

Dumped? By *her*? Nick hasn't been hanging out with us very long, but he's so far resisted every girl (and there have been lots) who's tried to pick him up. I've been assuming no one's good enough. But the girl I passed on the stairs, this Sarah chick, she was plain, pale, dressed in a jean jacket and jeans. Nothing extraordinary at all.

'I love her,' Nick says, fixing me with filmy, reddened eyes.

'Oh Nick —'

'I love her. I love her and she doesn't love me.' His shoulders start to shake. His beautiful face splits into cracks and fissures like an eighty-year-old man.

I put an arm around his shoulders, breathing his smells of leather and smoke and spicy soap, but he just folds up into himself more, so I quickly let go. In public school, there was a boy (one of the most popular boys there) who had the desk next to me one year. Any time I'd accidentally brush against him or his desk he'd go 'Ewww! Stevens touched me! Ewww! I got Stevens' germs!' And he'd rub at the spot going *bleck*, *ugh*, and so on. I tried being nice to him but it didn't help. So I tried telling him to grow up, but it didn't help. Finally I completely, utterly ignored him for the rest of the year. This

wasn't easy. But I did it: I pretended he didn't exist. If I had
to look in his direction to watch the teacher, I forced my eyes
not to drift sideways, where he'd be staring. When he spoke
to me I imagined being outside, anywhere else. Eventually, I
stopped hearing him at all.

Nick's sobs are shaking the bed. I wonder, though, if he
would cry like this if he wasn't Nick François, the adored god
whose every move is Important. Who never has to worry.
Then feel mean for thinking this.

'I love someone who doesn't love me,' Nick slurs through
his hands. 'I love someone, and they don't love me.'

**First almost boyfriend, somewhat drunk**
'I want you to suck me.'

Instead I kiss him again. Harder than I want to, given the
situation.

He pulls his mouth away and looks up at me. He says,
'Germaine, I want you to go down on me.'

'I can't *here*.'

'Yes you can. No one's watching.' His hand takes mine and
presses it to his crotch. I look around. True: no one's paying
attention. They're all talking up front in the seats, though this
I can only tell because their mouths and heads are moving.
The van's speakers, cranked on the Who, are right beside our
heads, and the noise, the inability to see outside, seems to cut
us off, tucked in our own dark cave on the foam mattress.

His hand's moving my fingers over his hardness. I start
squeezing, stroking. I estimate ten minutes, tops, till we reach
home. A hand job for five might be okay. If I lie on top of him
like we're necking no one will be able to tell.

'Germaine …'

'I can't. Not here.' I squeeze him harder.

......................................................................

'It's okay.' His hands come up and cup my face. 'It's
okay,' he repeats, stroking my hair. Fuck! I did it once, and
now look: I've created a monster. I should be a Barbie, he
could just pop my head off and put it on his cock. The rest of
me would sit up front.

The van hits a pothole and I topple off my elbow onto his
chest. My jaw clacks shut.

'Ow. Sorry.' Great, I can see the headline: YOUTH
DAMAGED BY SEX ACT IN MOVING VEHICLE.

'Germaine ...'

Maybe it's okay to give a guy head in a van full of people
as long as it's dark, there's music blasting, the people aren't
paying attention and the guy is almost my boyfriend? I try to
imagine what someone else would do: Regina, Debbie
Deering.

'Germaine ...'

Those pleading, childish eyes. How helpless guys become,
all because of this thing, hot and urgent under my fingers. I
bend and touch my lips to the exposed V of skin at the top of
his jacket zipper.

'Germaine ...'

'Shhhhh.' A child in my hands.

'Germaine ...'

Totally in my hands. I bend lower.


**Mike, sober**

'Fuck. I can't believe it.'

Regina shakes her head. 'I know,' she says softly.

'What did Pete say Mike said?'

'I don't think he said much. They were riding along, and
Mike asked Pete how things were going with him and me,
they talked about it, so then Pete asked Mike how things were

going with you two. And that's when he said it.'

'What, exactly?'

Regina shrugs. 'That you'd fucked.'

'And Pete believed him?'

'He didn't know. He thought it was possible.'

'Jesus Christ.'

From the bleachers we watch half a dozen runners pound around the track. Their breath rises in little clouds. Someone blows a whistle periodically. Behind the track lies the football field, black and craggy with melting snow. I'm avoiding the smoking pit for today. Maybe for a few days.

'Why didn't Pete say something sooner?' Pete is what Regina calls her 'fuck buddy,' although they don't technically fuck.

'I dunno. Until Cheryl started blabbing I guess he thought maybe you didn't want anyone to know, if it was true.'

'As if!' I shiver, the wood under our bums cold as metal. We watch the track.

Regina lights a smoke. Watching her cheeks get cute little dimples as she inhales, I wish it was her. Why do *I* have to deal with an asshole like Mike? Why can't it be Regina, who wouldn't even care what people said. Yet if it wasn't for her I'd probably never even meet guys. And Regina has other problems, like her weight ... I press my palm to my forehead, pushing the ugly thoughts away.

'The whole bloody school probably knows by now,' I say. 'They're so addicted to gossip here.' It's probably already starting, the association: Germaine Stevens, SLUT. A stain that'll fade but never die, because some asshole always keeps these kinds of things alive – so the sleazeball guys know who to go to, and the others to stay far away from. Impossibly far.

He dumped me last month. Almost boyfriend number two, who also lasted the big three weeks. Yesterday, this chick from

the twelfth grade named Cheryl, this skank with a bloated
face so layered in foundation and powder and eyeliner she
looks like a corpse, this witch who's never even *met* Regina or
me, slithers over to Regina out on the pit and starts blabbing.
About me. How she's dating Mike's best friend and heard me
and Mike have broken up. Oh, and heard we'd fucked. Like
this is a general topic of conversation now.

I should have figured. Anyone who says 'I love you' then
immediately tries to stick his dink up your snatch has got to
be a moron. Like those words are the equivalent of *Open
Sesame.* Excuse me, Mike, I wanted to say, there are some
things here to discuss. Like birth control. Or like the fact that
I've never fucked anyone. Oh, and BIRTH CONTROL, you
ass. No way was I ending up pregnant like Lizzy Rogers in
grade twelve. So I just kept my thighs closed – not difficult,
considering my jeans were barely down to my knees – and
pretended I didn't notice the head of Mike's cock going doink,
doink, doink, off my pubic bone every few seconds.

'We'll get him back,' Regina says. 'Start another rumour.
Punish the bastard.'

'Yeah.'

It won't matter, though.

Past the fence at the end of the football field are the backs
of houses. Houses surround MacKenzie, so despite the school
being built on the only hill in Greenview, there really is no
view – green or otherwise. Just the rooftops of more houses,
repeating like images in a mirror. That's all. Here, the rest of
the city, the rest of the world, don't exist.

### Debbie

On Valentine's Day people come around to hand out gifts. Not
to everyone, of course. You have to order them ahead of time

for whoever you want to send them to. The girls get roses, the guys, little plastic mesh bags of candy hearts. It's all kind of funny and twisted. Whenever a guy gets something, everyone goes *awww* and he turns red. That's the funny part. When a girl gets a rose she smiles, and all the other girls who never get anything feel like dogshit. Some of them don't even watch.

I watch because it's more interesting than class. The student council people give out the goods, dressed up in red clothes and baseball caps embroidered with the name CUPID. This year, when the girl calls Debbie's name no one's surprised. She looks very dainty going up to receive her flower, doing this little dip with her head and smiling shyly. She makes you feel happy for her, which is annoying.

The Cupid calls her name again.

There are a few gasps. Debbie does a little squeal, covers her face with her hands and blushes. She heads back up to the front to get her second rose. Our teacher grins with approval.

The Cupid calls her name again.

'Oh man,' I hear some guy say. Debbie. Debbie. Debbie. Bong, bong, Cupid keeps calling her name and piling on the flowers. Five times. Debbie, Debbie, Debbie, Debbie, Debbie, Debbie, Debbie. A dozen times. How sweet.

Debbie gets back in her desk with her armful of roses like a pageant queen. Through the rest of class I smell them. I feel their redness. Red for sweet sweet love. When she whispers to me I ignore her. If I don't, I'll vomit the *Fuck off and die forever, skank-faced, airhead, shit-for-brains cunt!* that's throbbing in my skull. I don't know why. After all, she's never done anything wrong.

### Gavin

'Jesus, check Regina out.'

I don't want to look, but I do. Regina's edging Gavin toward a corner — the farthest one in the rec room. Both wearing smiles, but Gavin's is more embarrassed while Regina's is naughty. She reaches up to grab his collar, wiggling her shoulders a bit, giggling, moving her notoriously large and firm breasts closer to his chest. All he can do is back up. Yet you can tell he knows he can't back up forever.

'Man,' Bono says, 'she just doesn't get it, does she?'

I smirk. I don't know what everyone else has noticed. I don't want to say too much.

'I mean, God,' Bono raises her hand a little drunkenly, lets it flop again on the cushion, 'like, it's kind of *obvious* the guy's not interested.'

I decide it's safe to agree.

Bono's head lolls on the back of the couch, her habitual baseball cap skewed sideways. She turns her face to me with a grin, her eyes knowing behind the lenses. She punches my thigh, hard. 'Yeah, not in her. Don't we know that Germaine, eh?' Thump thump. 'Eh?' Thumping harder. 'DON'T WE KNOW THAT EH GERMAINE?'

'Ow! Fuck off!' I lunge forward with my foaming beer, cap it with my mouth. Regina and Gavin look over.

After I get my beer in order I ask Bono what she means. I want to hear her say it, now that I know she knows. I want confirmation. But she's sulky that I snapped at her. She turns and talks to someone else.

There are suddenly just four of us left in the room and then Bono asks Jackie to go upstairs with her, leaving two: Gavin and me. Side by side on the couch. Regina's gone out for a toke. She tried to persuade Gavin to go, but only a little. It *is* pretty obvious now.

# A Short Chronicle of Tenth-Grade Love

....................................................................

'What are you thinking?' he asks, shifting closer. I smile.
Mick Jagger pleading *gimmee shelter* and every object in the
room abruptly snapping into focus. Gavin presses his lips to
my ear and mouths the question again, ultra slow. The
vibrations tickle, flutter along my limbs.

'It sounds like we're under water,' I say, laughing a little.

'Weee aaaaarrrrre,' he gurgles. Then he quickly slides over
so he's straddling my lap. Brings his mouth close to mine but
it's all too fast and I pull back. Imagining Regina coming
down the stairs, getting this slap in the face. Or someone else
who'll tell her, *Germaine stole your guy*. Except he's not hers.
She just saw him first, laid her claim. With Regina, though,
that's all that matters.

Gavin slides off and sits on the carpet, sipping his beer.
From this angle I can see down his shirt, the skin entering
shadows, a world I could curl into. A forbidden world. As I
get up to leave I reach out and smooth his hair with my palm.
One touch. I can at least take this with me.

We're all a bit wasted as we walk to the variety store. Twice
Gavin tugs at my arm, trying to get me to walk behind with him
or leave – I don't know what. But I don't. I just keep walking.
When he says goodbye to us, he doesn't look my way.

The next morning I wake up way too early. Light seeps
though the gauzy curtains. Even the concert posters on the
walls look grey. I lie for a couple of hours, trying to fantasize
about Gavin and me in the ravine, daydream myself into
feeling better, but it doesn't work. Why is it that some dreams
stop being imaginable?

## Debbie

The speeding car brakes. In the corner of my eye its

..................................................................

headlights brighten, and then the Trans Am's hood with its golden, wing-spread eagle cruises into view, stereo beating the air. After a moment there's the whir of an electronic window, and the music cuts to a deep voice.

'Hey.'

The way I play this game is to never look. Besides, I already know who it is. Main question is whether he's alone.

Tires crunch the tiny pebbles that have been plinking and skittering across the dried-up streets like beads, the last traces of winter sand trucks.

'*Hey.*'

Tony. Hot Tony. I turn my head. He's alone. Silhouette of thick hair against the pale light of lawn lamps, one arm slung across the wheel.

'Hi.'

'How's it goin'?'

'Fine.' I look away. I've walked half a block since he arrived but it's a long way home yet. My breath a pale cloud, like smoke. Is it really possible that I can feel the engine's heat on my face? I feel something.

'It's Gurmaine, right?'

'Germaine.'

'*Gerrr*maine,' he says, savouring the sound. 'Yeah. I've noticed you.' He pauses, either expecting a reply or letting this statement have its amazing effect. 'You're hard not to notice, you know?' he says.

The music ends. The plastic click of a cassette being popped from its case reminds me of the clink of Debbie's engagement ring when she rested her hand on her desk. It's gone now, the ring. Debbie dumped Tony because he was becoming 'too possessive.' Plus Kevin Traynor, the richest, sportiest, supposedly cutest wet dream of every chick at

MacKenzie, was dying to take her out.

'So where you goin'? Can I give you a drive?' Tony asks. Not the same Tony that Debbie knew – no way. This one's the same but not the same. It's scary how people are like that, the same and different all the time, with each person they meet, and how shocked everyone is that this happens when they realize it. But if they just took a look at themselves they'd stop being surprised. Here's me alone with babe Tony, for instance, but I'm not into it. His creeping car and dumb-ass lines make me feel cranky and tired and a bit sorry for him.

'It's okay. I don't have far.'

'Well, why don't you stop walking so fast for a second and come inside.'

I glance at the car's dashboard glow, the warm, crinkly leather seats where Debbie got all those hickeys. I screw my mouth up. I don't know if I want to laugh or spit.

'No thanks,' I say.

Pop go the pebbles under the tires. The Trans Am's engine's a bit chokey and I wonder if Tony's ever been turned down and what kind of girl would find his black lair and tough-guy orders exciting. Of course Debbie didn't get the trailing car in the dark. Debbie got the roses. Debbie got love.

Tony softens his voice. 'I don't bite.'

I flash a polite smile. 'I'm really fine. Thanks.' And suddenly I'm plunging forward, it seems, because the car's pulled back. Then the squeal of brakes on rubber, and a rush that leaves one word floating, flung into the frosty night as two angry red eyes disappear down the street: BITCH.

..........................................................

# Thaw

Another crap Saturday in March when the day's as grey as a
school hallway, the sun a dull fluorescent bulb behind the
clouds. Thawing but still freezing cold. The path above the
river's tricky. Boggy, pocked with heel holes. I pick my steps
carefully behind Bono, hunching my shoulders against the
damp (though it doesn't work) and wishing she'd say
something. She walks a steady beat, like she's not afraid of
slipping.

The path cuts the side of the ravine. A couple of feet away,
the ground scarps down almost straight to the river. One bad
step and you're a goner. The snow might stop you, but
probably not. And there's no ice left to land on at the bottom.
Not solid ice, that's all broken now, turned brown and slushy
by the water and rushing away with all the other crud, the
mud, the branches, everything that died this winter. The
neighbourhood's all dog-shit snow puddles and rot stink.
Swimming pools like forgotten fishbowls, gooey with green
slime and dead frogs whose waterlogged skins break apart in
the skimmers. The river's the worst of all. In summer, when
it's so clear you can spot crayfish scooting across the bottom, I
always forget it can look this ugly.

Something's caught my eye on the opposite shore. I call out
to Bono.

..............................................................

'Hey, did you see that?'

'What?' She doesn't turn.

'Over there, in the trees.' A flash of orange in the grainy black and white, I thought, but now I'm not sure I saw anything. Maybe I just wanted to, to break the silence. Bono stops and looks briefly at the trees. She doesn't speak, only turns her head and gives me the eye. I'm not prepared, and she sees me with my mouth open, a worried look on my face. Her expression – would you call it sly? I flip this over in my mind as we go on. Heads, no. Tails, you bet. She's been practically my best friend since grade six – since before Regina, at least – but I still don't know what she'll do if she realizes I've bullshitted her. Either she knows or doesn't. Everything else makes sense from there.

I'd acted pissed off when she arrived. A good angle, going for sympathy. 'My fucking parents are making me go out with them tonight for my grandmother's birthday,' I'd said.

'Grannie's birthday?' Bono made a face.

I rolled my eyes.

'That sucks.'

'Yeah.' I zipped up my jacket. Opened the screen door and squeezed onto the slippery driveway, Dad's Buick too close to the house again. Mission accomplished. There. Right there I should have left it. But I didn't. I lie all the time – to save myself from looking stupid, getting into shit. Not this kind of thing, though. Standing up a friend. As if I have enough of those to do that. I thought Bono would see through it in a second.

'Yeah,' I went on, 'I'm really sorry about tonight. Too bad there's nothing I can do,' and blah screwing-it-up-big-time blah. Then as if that wasn't enough, I *looked* at her. She was in the doorframe right behind me so I had to crane and twist

..........................................................

my neck. I thought I was giving her a good face – a
combination of pissed-off and pity-me. But something else
slipped in. At least, it may have. Bono frowned, a squint
behind her steamed-up glasses. I felt a little tug in the air
between us, like a jolt of electricity.

'Hey, whatever,' she said. 'It's no biggie.'

We splashed up the empty gloomy street, where everyone
had their lights on inside.

True, it's not my fault. Regina had set up the double date,
and if I'd said no I would have wrecked everything. Her
words keep telling me to chill: *If Bono wants to be that way
it's her problem. How can she blame you?* Problem. I'd never
quite thought of Bono that way – as having one. Still, it's not
like Bono and I don't hang together all the time, for fuck's
sake. Yes I promised to come over tonight but we had no great
plans, just the same as always – lying around her living room
listening to tunes, reading out lyrics we already know by
heart while her nutzo cat claws the carpet. Sneak a few inches
from her mother's fresh bottle of Scotch, then argue over
whether to watch *Baretta* or *Kolchak: The Night Stalker.*
Bono doesn't need me for that.

If she was in my place she'd ditch me the same way.
Except that's impossible. Her being in my place, that is –
lined up with a guy.

We stop where the path dives into the woods, a steep slope
that's always gouged with bike tracks in the summer. The soft
ground's dark, soaked full like a sponge and streaked with
boot skids – skids running shiny smooth to little twists of
mud, where the feet tripped. Here and there are black mucky
holes from elbows, knees, fists.

'Fucking great,' I say. There's no other way down, the trees alongside offer nothing to grab onto.

'Well,' Bono smiles, and starts backing up on the path. 'Looks like we gotta make a run for it!'

'You're not –' But she's already doing it: pounding past me and taking off, leaping God knows how in her parka and boots. She easily clears the mud slick but not the entire slope. Thumps down on her feet with a splat and skids with knees bent and arms spread like a surfer, then pulls up safe.

She puts her hands on her hips, breathing hard. Grins, flashing bright front teeth that are too white in spots, I suppose because she's always picking at the enamel with her thumbnail. 'Your turn, German,' she calls. Because she knows what I'm thinking she adds, 'It's *easy*.'

I want to believe her. But I've fallen (ha ha) for that before. Yeah, I'm sure it's easy – for Bono. But I've never known what it's like, this feeling or knowledge that your body will do the right thing for you, obey you. The athlete's feeling. Bono's always had it.

I calculate the slope. Fifteen, twenty feet? If I were alone I'd squat and waddle down. I know this looks stupid but I really don't feel like falling. I'm not scared, I'm just sick of it. Falling. I've been falling my whole life. My bony bruised shins and knees are ongoing diaries of what I fuck up trying to do. The thing about strong, co-ordinated people like Bono is they believe it's nothing special. For them, it's just being *normal*. When I first met Bono in grade six, I couldn't do anything. She was already talked about then, the girl who looked and acted like a boy, slouched low in her desk and never wore a dress, not even jewellery. Yet these were only whispers, because unlike me, Bono never got taunted. She taught me bike skids, how to catch crayfish. We tore through the neighbourhood on our bikes after dark, hollering obscenities.

............................................................................

We launched graffiti attacks on the school. She was the
coolest girl I'd ever met.

But I'm still a spaz. I take a run and as I'm about to leave
the ground I see Bono already starting to laugh.

Of course I go down. But not too badly. At least I manage
to catch myself on my hands (I pulled my mitts off first) and
keep my jeans clean. 'You jumped too far back,' she says,
shaking her head. She's always giving me advice, like she's
my coach.

I put snow on my stinging hands. 'Where to?' We didn't
have a plan when we left my place, just the usual – getting
away from my parents, who were rearranging the dining room
to fit in their thrilling new buffet. Bono's place was off-limits
too. And in Greenview, our retarded little suburb stuck on the
edge of town, if you don't have a car to get out this leaves
only two places: the variety store, or the ravine.

Bono smirks. 'Well, I was going to save this for tonight,
when you came over …'

I keep wiping my hands. Someone told me once that you
can spot liars by the way they fidget. The body language. The
stupid body.

'But since you're *not* …' She pauses and yanks her mitts
off with her teeth, one then the other, and clamps them
between her knees. Her big hands are criss-crossed with
scabby scratches from playing rough with her cat. '… then
we'll just have to have it now,' she says, feeling in her
pockets. Suddenly she cuffs her fist to my face like she's going
to punch me. I'm used to this bad joke, Bono's reminder that
she could demolish me in a second, so I've trained myself over
the years not to react. But today the thought *she knows* makes
me jump.

There's a ball of tinfoil between her thumb and forefinger.

'Doob!' I say, almost too happily. 'Right on.'

Bono puts the wad back in her pocket.

'Where should we smoke it?'

She puckers her lips as if thinking. As if. The coin flips in my head but won't land. Bono's too careful to see through. She's the one with the body that does what she wants.

She begins walking away and calls over her shoulder: 'Dead Man's Creek.'

At home I have a letter from Bono that she wrote the summer before we started high school. She was visiting her dad's house in Alberta.

Dear German,

So how are you. I am fine. Well enough of that shit, have you gotten high lately. You know, you are a degenerate slob, sleazy pothead and I don't know how Alvie and Cassy stand someone as disgusting as you living in their house but of course they are even worse. Have you checked out the fort lately or have you just been masturbating. Don't do it too much or there'll be nothing left for all the guys you're going to lay at MacKenzie, you slut.

My dad's place is OK. I miss you so much and if you don't write me back I'll come and shove a baseball bat up you when I get home. I know you're dying without me so I'll try not to come back covered in cow shit unless you want to pick it off.

Your enemy forever, Bono

# Thaw

What drives me nuts about most girls is how *nice* they pretend to be. They're so serious about it that even when they're trying to make you cry, they act like it's because they're offended that you're not nice. Not pretty, not dressed right, hitting the volleyball right, whatever. Of course they're offended! You know you're hideous!

Bono isn't like most girls. I don't think it's mean to say that, except for her body, she isn't really a girl at all.

We follow the river path then take the fork that veers into the woods. In a couple of places I spot dog pee, but it looks old. Winding along the river for miles, the ravine's the only place in Greenview where you can get away from houses, but pretty well the only people who come down here are kids. I suspect that most adults here don't even know about the ravine (since they can't see it from their cars), or anyway don't know how to get down into it through the back of the public school's field or from the trail that starts between two houses on McKay Crescent. And if they did know, would they care?

As the river noise fades, Bono finally starts talking. She tells me how she lifted the buds off her brother Trent – aka the Mummy, because he doesn't talk and seems to have no brain left. Is Trent a dealer? This is the great mystery we've been trying to solve for years. The odds are high (ha ha), but there's never any hard proof, except for the fact that he makes minimum wage at his weekend dish washing job, yet owns a totally hot '69 Mustang. But the weirdest thing is how Trent acts around Bono. About three years ago, Trent stopped speaking to her – ever. We're talking total avoidance of contact. This isn't hard in Bono's house: with her dad remarried in Alberta and her mom working the evening shift at Bell and looking for a new husband on the weekends, no one eats together or anything. Trent's room is in the basement, Bono's upstairs. They get dinner from the Crock Pot, a steamy mash their mom leaves simmering before she goes to work.

So. Bono spies Trent tossing his jean jacket on the couch as he's getting ready to go out after the usual ten-word phone call, and she makes a beeline. Sits right beside it. Almost on top of it, holding a textbook open on her lap with one hand, feeling with the other. Sure enough, when Trent comes out of the can his mouth opens and he's so terrified to see her that he forgets what he's doing and automatically veers away into the kitchen. This gives Bono just enough time to finish rifling through the loose change, matchbooks, breath freshener rolls, slips of paper with phone numbers, Visine, rolling paper packs, safety pins and beer caps crammed in his jacket pockets until she's found the clear plastic baggie with its spongy load. The Mummy reappears, mumbling: 'Uh, hey man, I uh, need my jacket.' Whoa. Trent makes a whole sentence. Must have exhausted him.

Our laughter echoes in the empty woods. I decide Bono must have believed my grandmother story, otherwise she wouldn't be having fun with me.

Bono says Trent's a perma-stoned freak. That's the only way to explain his behaviour – paranoia. She throws up her hands. Even the way she does this is completely not-like-a-girl. It's a jab, a smack. Like there's an invisible thing she's batting away. Bono always seems about to beat the crap out of something, though she never does. Even in her walk, she swings her arms extra hard – whack whack! I think, Trent's not just a freak, he's *freaked out*. At her, his sister.

Her clothes are all boys'. Under her turtleneck and baggy shirt, her boobs are braless. Her shoulders curve, permanently slouched like she's trying to pull in her chest, stop its growth. Her favourite show's *Starsky and Hutch*. She's hot for guys (*You should see the cowboy next to my dad's, German, what a butt!*), but she's never kissed one. Regina and I have tried to think of possible romantic candidates. Bono comes to parties and won't leave our side. The guys edge away.

Recently, a goofus in one of my classes told me he'd heard Bono pees standing up.

There's no precedent, like she came from nowhere. In her family, Bono looks adopted or hospital-switched: her mother, Faye, is all nicotine-yellow skin and tiny bones. Her sisters look like sisters. But who could be Bono's real relatives? I've seen some possible distant cousins – like Barbara Marsh, who in public school once threw a shot-put ball across the patio and injured the principal. But even though Barbara's six-foot-one and built like a football player, she still acts and dresses like a girl. With Bono, it's not just that she's stronger than average. It's as if she's a different *species*. From one of those prehistoric branches that went off on its own, like the duckbilled platypus. We're fifteen now. Trent isn't the only one who can't handle it.

The meadow's white with brown dead grass poking through. Everything looks sunken, as if the snow's melting from the inside out. Ahead, the trees surrounding the creek stand like spindly wet roots. A crow rises from one of them and flaps slowly into the clouds, like it can do whatever the hell it wants.

Why it's called Dead Man's Creek I've never found out. Kids call it that, ones who know the ravine. But there are connections. There's the rusted and weedy old milk truck at the edge of the creek, below one of the steepest walls of the

ravine. We pass its spooky black windows on the way. All four
wheels rest on the ground like it's getting ready to drive off
across the snow and make a delivery. But there aren't any
roads nearby, never have been.

There's the dead kids, the ones who've drowned in the
river near the bluffs. South where the creek drains and the
river curves west, the opposite shore rises high, sandy and
spotted with perfectly round black holes that nest swallows.
Here the riverbed gets deep. The undertow's a surprise. I felt
it once myself, treading water when I spilled off our raft. It
felt like I'd caught my foot in a vacuum.

There's also the story of an Indian graveyard somewhere
near the creek. But there's always one of those, and no one
seems to know any details.

We're just in the woods when Bono grabs my arm. 'Hey!'
she whispers. 'Up ahead. Check it out.'

Through the slimy-looking trunks and branches we can see
The Rocks: two massive boulders dumped by a glacier when
the ravine was carved out. I've been assuming this is where
Bono's heading. They're graffitied over with skulls and
crossbones, and make a good hangout spot. Except that two
guys are leaning against one of them.

Bono peers through her foggy lenses. 'Who is it?'

If they're public-school boys we can kick them off. But
they don't look young. One of them, I can see, has a thick
moustache and whiskers. Not guys at all, then. Men. They're
dressed in jeans and running shoes, boxy ski jackets, wool
toques. We can tell they don't live in Greenview. The way
their hair scraggles out from under the wool. The tears in
their mud-splashed coats.

'What the fuck are they doing here?' Bono says.

'Shhh! How should I know?' Greenview has nothing to

attract strangers, much less anyone cool who's unfortunate enough to be born here. The guys are huddled together, fiddling with something between their hands.

'Probably pervs,' Bono whispers. 'Or pigs.' Cops invade us sometimes in the summers, driving their squad cars onto the school tarmac then hiking all the way through the field and down into the woods to bust bush parties.

'They don't look like pigs,' I say. 'How'd they find the trail? Let's go back to the river.'

'Do you have a light?'

'No. I forgot my smokes.'

'Then we'll have to make friends,' Bono grins, '"cause I forgot matches.'

'What – ask them?'

Bono elbows me in the ribs. She's almost jolly. 'Why not? What, you nervous or something?'

I twist away. Her pokes are always too hard, her kidding-around shoulder punches too rough. Like we're guy-to-guy. She's probably lying about the matches to bug me, to get me back.

'Let's forget it,' I say.

She kicks my boot. 'Don't be such a wuss! Besides,' she adds in a sing-song, happy voice, 'it's your grannie's birthday! We should celebrate, right?'

So she knows.

She goes and leaves me feeling vile, like some rotted thing finally broken open. *I'll come and shove a baseball bat up you when I get home.*

I wait behind a tree. I wouldn't talk to those sleazeballs anywhere. Plus I have another problem: imagining how Bono will destroy me.

When they hear her, one quickly pockets something. She walks up to them swinging her body with the cool-dude, ghetto-cowboy stride I think she must have seen on TV. I always think Bono must be something she's seen somewhere, that there's no way she could have made herself up being born in Greenview. Her parka hides her hips, flattens her chest. She wears Kodiak workboots. Even her glasses are neutral-looking. Her hood covers her long hair and with this one female trait hidden, the face looking out could be anything.

The guys react to Bono the way all guys seem to: like unfriendly dogs. First there's nothing. They see a lone guy who's obviously not big enough to be any trouble. Then something catches, a strange scent. They blink. They sniff. Whoa! What kind of guy's this? They glare, prickling all over (one of them actually pauses with a lit match mid-air). It looks like they're going to attack, but something saves her in time. Maybe the voice, which is higher than mine. Maybe some loose strands of hair. The guys clue in: a chick! What's more, a totally unfuckable chick – not even a dog, man. Just a complete nonentity.

More or less friendly now they pass Bono matches, but instead of leaving she waves me forward. Bitch. Now it looks like I've been hiding. When the men see me approach their reaction isn't at all the same. They stare at me hard the whole time.

Bono throws back her hood and rolls the joint. She wets the paper with the tip of her tongue. I watch her and the guys watch me, waiting for our little toke party to begin.

I can see how old they are now, in their thirties, maybe forties. Skin bags under the eyes. One has deep creases beside his mouth and grey hairs in his moustache. He raises his chin at me. 'Hey, what's your name?'

Oh God, here we go. I'm sure they haven't asked Bono *her* name.

'Germaine,' I say. I do my polite-but-not-too-friendly smile.

'Germaine,' he nods, his mouth curling on one side. Dark eyes cruise down my body. Why did I wear tight jeans? Stupid question: they're all I have. 'I'm Ted,' the guy says. 'This is Will. You have a pretty name, Germaine.'

I thank him. Turn the smile down a notch.

Bono has the joint going. She takes a toke and holds it out. 'You guys want some?'

'Sure,' they say. Of course. Ugly bastards, they're clearly already fried. Or something. Bloodshot eyes, and a smell like sour beer.

We huddle around the rock and pass the joint. I don't take much. I don't want to share spit with guys who have dark brown stains on their pants and stare at me like they're imagining all sorts of stuff they'd like to do. I can feel it, especially from the moustached one, this Ted. Like I'm being shut inside one of his glossy magazines: a slut in a short skirt with no underwear and a shaved pussy, the bikini-wearing virgin schoolgirl next door who won't do it but gets so incredibly hot as you help her with the suntan lotion that she ends up begging for it on all fours.

The joint goes around. Ted and Will take crackling hauls that turn the heater into a bright red eye. They suck the smoke into their lungs and hold it until they get teary and start to choke.

Ted stares at my legs again – more specifically, my crotch. His silence as he does this makes it worse. 'So where you guys from?' I ask.

They bust up laughing. Laugh loud, wheezily.

'We could ask you the same question,' Will finally says, grinning. He has a red pudgy face and wears wire-rimmed spectacles that seem wrong, like someone's tried to make him look smarter.

'We live around here,' I say.

'That so? Well, you could say we're just passing through.' He glances at Ted, who smirks. I look at Bono. She's grinning, but in a nervous way. It makes her look more like a girl.

Ted passes the joint and I drop it. The snow kills it with a little piff. I dig it out from the shallow hole, hand it back to Ted. His index finger scrapes mine during the exchange.

Will remarks on the good quality of the dope. We chat about it for a bit, about dope in general.

Melting snow drips. Way on the edge of hearing is another sound, a trickling so faint it makes my ears itch: creek water.

'So,' says Ted, holding his palm open to Will, who smacks a roach clip in it, 'what are two girls like yourselves doing today?'

'Meeting friends,' I lie. A whole troupe of them, I want to add. Coming right now. Coming around the corner right now.

Ted's lips harden under his snot-damp moustache. 'Friends, eh?' I nod. He frowns. 'Well, what are *we* then?'

Bono and I laugh. Ted doesn't. It seems to be a serious question.

I don't know what to say. Even Bono's face is bright beacon red like it always gets when she's embarrassed.

A chill stiffens my neck. I have a lot of memories of situations like this. In public school, some tough kid starts in, and no matter what you say back it's insulting. Like the pretty girls – you offend them just by being alive. You make a statement even when you say or do nothing. Your body says it

74

for you: says you're a loser, ugly, sucky, freaky. Since I started
high school mine's been saying different things, especially to
guys, but they're never quite the right things, the things that
make guys hold your hand or want to walk with you after
school. I don't know what these are. I don't have the code.

The wet is worse off the path. Water's been leaking
through the seam of my left boot, my fingers are stiff and blue
from having my mitts off to smoke up. Blip, blip-blip, goes
the creek. My jacket creaks as I shift on my legs, trying to
warm my toes. I want to look at Will, to see his goofy smile
lighten things up, but Ted won't take his eyes off me. This
isn't the first time I've wished I was a guy. It's about the
zillionth time. A guy, or someone like Bono.

'Well, these are people we hang out with all the time,' I
finally say.

Ted seems even angrier. He spits on the ground. 'So what
do you got against new friends?'

'Nothing.' I try to smile. Down boy. 'Nothing at all.'

Ted opens his hands, sweeping them in front of him. 'Then
spend the day with us,' he says. 'We'll be your friends.'

All I can do is smile.


The joint's gone (they smoked most of it). The last pot smell
flits away. I make small talk. I say it was great meeting them.
I say we're sorry but we have to get going, we have plans and
our friends will be waiting. I feel like an idiot, especially for
saying the word 'friends' with Ted's invitation hanging in the
air, in the middle of our circle, untouched. Ted digs into the
snow with his heel, frowning. The hole quickly goes down to
black.

'Well, see you.' I wave, edging away.

They still say nothing. Bono and I start back down the

path, her in front. The woods seem to narrow. My back feels
wide open. Bono's too slow and no one knows we're here.
The river is swift.

*Don't run.* He can see my ass, full view. Shouldn't have
bought a bomber-style jacket, shouldn't have worn these
jeans. Like an invitation. It's my fault. That's what he thinks.
Maybe even what Bono thinks.

We round the bend and the meadow opens up ahead through
the trees. Then we hear it. Ted's voice through the woods.

'Hey Germaine!'

I keep moving. I know what's coming.

'Come back and sit on my face!'

'Holy shit,' Bono mutters.

'Hey Germaine! I want to fuck your snatch!'

Bono starts giggling. 'Come *on*,' I say, and shove past. My
armpits are prickly and damp. I start to jog. Sprint. Out from
under the trees. Running past the truck hollowed out like a
skull, my boots sliding on mud, rubber slapping wet. My ears
filter the noise, listening for something else.

What comes is Ted's voice, shouting through the ravine for
the last time. *You fucking cunt-faced bitch!* Words as clear as
a rifle-shot crack.

Being cold has different levels. First is the outer kind, where
it's just your skin. You shiver, get goosebumps. It goes away
soon enough. When it's worse the cold seeps into your limbs.
You come home and the warmth burns. Your hands scream
like they've forgotten anything but a deep freeze.

My cold is the next level: everywhere. My lungs feel like
rubber bottles filled with ice water. I lift leadweight legs
through the woods. I can't even be bothered to put my hands
in my pockets.

Bono says, 'Wow, that was weird.'

Fuck her.

'Where do you think they were they from?'

'Don't know.'

Her parka makes a swishy noise behind me. I try to walk faster. On my feet, I guess, though they seem only imaginary.

'Germaine, stop rushing!' Bono says. 'No one's coming.'

'I'm freezing.'

She comes alongside. Her loping walk. Swish-swish. I check behind us and she's right, the path's clear, the meadow a receding white shine through the trees. Still, they might just be waiting.

Bono chuckles. 'He sure liked you.'

No jokes. 'You're the one who wanted to talk to them,' I say.

'Hey! We needed a light.'

'No we didn't. I said we should turn back.' I decide not to also point out that the light cost us most of her dope.

'Yeah, well.' Bono shrugs. 'Nothing happened.'

'As if that makes it okay! They might still come after us.' I doubt this now, but I want her to be scared. Or at least serious. But Bono never is, her general reaction to everything is to laugh. You fell down and sliced your knee. Oh ha ha ha. You like a guy. Oh ha ha ha. I wouldn't be *able* to tell her about tonight even if I wasn't breaking plans with her to begin with. 'Ohhh, a double date,' she'd sneer. 'How cute! Will you hold hands? Will you share a milkshake?' And so on.

Bono points her mitt at me. 'They might come after you, you mean.'

'Us.'

'No,' she grins, but can't stop her cheeks flushing red, 'I don't think so.' A short, choked laugh escapes her, and then it hits me that she knows everything: knows she's fumbling, arms and legs flailing – slipping away from us, away from everyone, the lies and bullshit from assholes like me just pushing her faster, further, out of control.

We scramble up the muddy slope. I want to be out of the woods, back on the path along the river, going home.

Walking single file, Bono in front again. The sky's darker. In a few hours I'm supposed to meet Regina. We're going to walk to Pete's, whose parents are in Florida. A whole house with Pete and Regina and me and Pete's friend Kirk, who has the most amazing long hair and sexy lower lip.

I don't care.

The river rushes below us. Swollen and broken, whisking things along. In the summer, the water's so low you can wade across in your sneakers in spots. For years Bono and I have spent summer holidays making forts in the ravine, building rafts from found plywood and floating downstream. If we passed boys on the shore they'd pelt us with stones but they were losers, they never made anything. We always talked about building a real raft and sailing as far as we could go, out of Greenview, past the bluffs, past downtown, into the country.

Back then, I thought Bono was the coolest, toughest, funnest girl I'd ever met. She was. And I was some skinny-armed loser.

I can see houses at the end of the path. The houses mean heat. A hot bath, and later there'll be excitement waiting. I think about steamy water. I think about kissing Kirk. I feel cold all over yet I want to say to Bono, wait. Wait here. Can't we just wait here?

# Clear Blue

The week my brother left there were UFOS in the sky. I wanted to call him but he was still on the road somewhere, chugging through the Rockies with his shit-box K-car crammed full. Even if he pretended otherwise I knew Ian would believe me, and he'd kill himself that something this astronomic had happened in Greenview – Land of the Walking Dead – and right in our own back yard on the day he'd driven off. Mr I Am So Cool, moving to Vancouver.

Last July. The best month of the year because the sun's at its closest and school its farthest. I was all ready to go with him, too. Just because I'm sixteen doesn't mean I don't deserve a vacation like the rest of them, and we hadn't taken a family trip since I was twelve. Mom and Dad even agreed to fly me home from B.C. They were surprised when I proposed going, but within minutes they were nodding and glancing at each other in their ESP way to verify they were on the same brainwave. Calculating that enough days in Ian's aura might actually fix me – as if he'd be tutoring me in math as we floored it on the TransCanada, or shouting sermons on the dangers of friends like Regina over Frank Zappa's rhyming obscenities. Ian, despite all the shit he'd driven Mom and Dad nuts with, was now newly sanctified, perfected, all because of a scholarship. When they finally said yes I whooped and ran around the house gathering road maps, travel guides, picture books of northern Ontario and the Banff National Park. I took out my spanking new driver's licence and looked at the photo. First item on the shopping list: cool shades.

But Numb Nuts refused to take me.

The morning he was leaving I lay on the rec room's sectional and ate my way through a package of crackers, watching dust motes swirl in the thin sunbeams falling through the grass-level windows. Overhead, Dad and Ian thudded boxes. The screen door made a springy *whee!* A pause, then BANG. It couldn't be propped open because of flies, though they got in anyway, found their way down into the gloom and furiously buzzed, butting against the windows above me. No one came and made me help. When it was finally quiet overhead I panicked that Ian had gone. I lunged up the stairs and outside but his car was still by the curb, the doors open and Ian's skinny calves jutting out the driver's side. Across the street Mr MacIntyre was mowing his lawn, which he does twice weekly in summer, and eyeing the boxes stacked by the wheels as if they were contraband – probably thinking Ian had been kicked out, and I wasn't far behind. The Stevens kids with their messy hair and cigarettes and smirks. I stared him down as I approached the car.

Ian wriggled out. Stray pieces of his ponytailed hair clung to his forehead, and his Godzilla Eats Wellington T-shirt was darkly sweat-stained down the front and back. He glanced my way, then hefted another box by his feet. Wedging this in the back seat, he said, 'You still don't believe me, do you? It's not going to be a sight-seeing trip, Germaine. It's not the way to see Canada. I'll be on the road nine or ten hours a day. Camping at night.'

'I love camping.'

'You've never *been* camping,' he grunted, his back to me. The car jiggled. It was an ugly old thing with pale spots where the paint was missing, like it had some kind of creeping disease. Still, it *was* a car. Tape player, built-in lighter, fuzzy red seat covers and a Canadian flag bumper sticker with a dope leaf in the middle and the words United Hempire Loyalist.

'Going to Arbor Lake Park five miles from here doesn't count,' Ian was saying. 'Where I'm going there'll be no showers. No curling iron.'

'Fuck off.'

Mr MacIntyre, who'd just switched off the mower, looked up quick.

'Sorry,' Ian said to me, emerging and reaching for another box labeled WINTER SWEATERS, ETC. in Mom's writing. He was laughing and tried to hide it.

'Right. I guess you'll be trapping and skinning your own dinner then?'

Ian rolled his eyes and sighed the way our parents do whenever I argue, as if talking with me is the most exhausting thing imaginable. I know it's just a tactic for avoiding the truth – which is that they can do whatever they want, and I must do what they tell me. The fact that Ian was even out of bed before noon was miraculous, more evidence that he'd become a Real Person. It seemed to happen instantly, the day last spring when he got the letter from the university. He quit his bartending job and his band. I came home from school and there they were: Ian and our parents, on the living-room couch drinking champagne. I thought I'd walked into the Twilight Zone. Ian still looked like a character from *The Freak Brothers* comics, my grinning parents were as goofy as ever, but the two sides had blended into some weird unity.

Ian had finished loading. He put his hands on his hips
(just like Dad!) and looked at me. 'It's just won't be fun,
that's all,' he said. 'But you can come visit whenever you want.
Maybe next summer. I'll show you around town. It'll be
much better than coming now.' He touched my arm and
started moving toward the house. Mr MacIntyre was watching
us as he raked sparse shavings of grass. 'Come with me,' Ian
said, his tone gentle now. 'I have to say goodbye to Mom and
Dad.'

Sure. Driving across Canada, through big-sky plains
toward those Rocky Mountain peaks spearing the mist like
something from *The Lord of the Rings* – not fun. Not at all.
And staying in Greenview to hang around the variety store
and watch morons monitor 1.5-inch lawns equals a fucking
laugh riot.

The first thing I did after Ian drove off was go downstairs and
ransack his stuff. In the furnace room he'd left behind a ton
of crap to be shipped to Vancouver, boxes of clothes and
books, years' worth of *Rolling Stone, Scientific American,
High Times* and *OMNI* issues. Under the bulb's dim light I
spent the afternoon making two piles: things I wanted and
things I might want. When I was done I realized they were
really just one pile of mediocre shit. Ian had taken everything
worth having: the carved wooden box with dope dust in its
corners, the cross-legged Buddha incense burner, the best
albums, the pedestal globe.

Sometime after my parents went to bed I headed out to the
back yard for a smoke. I usually walk around the crescent or
sit on the curb in front of our house to give the MacIntyres a
thrill, but this time I wanted to lie down on the grass – like I
should have been, by the shore of some Northern Ontario lake

..............................................................

where Ian was probably stoking a fire that moment. The night
was still humid, but the grass cool and prickly against my
legs. I lit my cigarette, glanced up at the Big Dipper. A silver
ball shot across it.

When I finally stumbled back inside, my throat burned
from chain smoking half a pack. I gulped a huge glass of milk
then went up to my room and sat on the bed in the dark,
staring out the window. Ian's going to choke, I thought. That
was no asteroid. Asteroids don't look like large metallic discs.
Asteroids don't fly around for half a hour, hovering and
changing direction in mid-flight, banking south, north, then
west. Finally disappearing west. I pressed my face to the
window and scanned the dark houses below, full of sleeping
bodies who didn't know that the sky was alive. It had given
itself away.

That was no asteroid. Ian was going to choke.

I called Regina and we started our vigil in my back yard the
next night. Mom and Dad had all the windows open because
of the heat, but their back bedroom has a cranky air
conditioner that gives good cover for talking. We set up Ian's
old pup tent, which reeked of armpits and putrid feet. Inside
we hunched in our bras and cut-offs and burned cone after
cone of patchouli incense. 'What's that smell?' Mom called,
her voice going all high and shaky at the end. Through the
mesh screen she appeared on the lawn like a gigantic white
grub with her nightie and pale limbs. She parted the flap and
peeked into the flashlit haze like there might be wild beasts
she'd have to tame.

'DOPE!' I said, and presented the incense box. We doubled
over laughing when she'd left. *Ganja! Doob! God help me
Mary Jane!*

.........................................................

My parents' air conditioner rattled, the Blacks' pool filter burbled and hummed next door. Down along the block, house lights shut off. Darkness moved in. Once the stars were visible we slid the sleeping bags half out of the tent. Sweaty, gasping in relief. That whole week the sky was clear. Right overhead, it seemed, the Big Dipper spread itself out. I told Regina the names of the planets in order from the sun. Mars the Red, with its two mini-moons. Gaseous Jupiter. Ian taught me this stuff years ago. He loved to make me recite things, words I didn't even know the meaning of, like 'logical fallacy'. I was his little protégé, he said. Not that I knew what that meant either.

Regina giggled. 'So what's it like on Uranus?'

'A fucking paradise,' I said.

Neither Regina's nor my parents have figured out that summertime backyard camping isn't about being able to blab all night. It's about setting up a tent, waiting until the parental units are zonked, then high-tailing it out of the yard. Then you can meet up with guys, or if there aren't any, roam around. Out here on the edge of the city, no one except high-school kids is up past midnight on a weekday. Sometimes you'll meet others walking or on bikes or cruising in cars, or gathered at certain places – the mulberry-tree grove in the public-school yard, or behind the store. But mostly the neighbourhood's empty, still, the world outside an echo. The streets bend round and round, a shell spiralling in on itself. Along the crescents and cul-de-sacs, lawn lampposts cast small, phosphorescent pools of light, marking the houses in the gloom. The shadows are friendly, let you climb fences and go pool-hopping, easily escape from snapped-on bedroom lights. You can even run down the middle of the street butt naked, which Regina and I did once, clutching our clothes,

..............................................................

her boobs bouncing like molded Jell-O and our feet slapping
concrete, singing *The night time / Is the right time / For
LOOOOVE!*

But for our UFO vigil, I made Regina promise we'd stay in
my yard. I wanted a witness, and besides, I said, what was
happening in that sky was more wild than anything in
Greenview. Regina lay on her back. Her cigarette pulsed red
above her face like the landing light of a plane. She sighed
with boredom and said, 'Germ, whip down your pants. The
aliens will mistake it for the moon.'

We did have dope – a dry turd lump of hash – but didn't
fire it up because I said we needed to be straight. We propped
ourselves on our elbows and craned our necks, staring. Stars
arced across the sky, some gleaming like new metal – Polaris
and Thubar. Others duller, colder, older. And behind these
were the rest, the zillions, so faint they flickered, as if the sky
were rippling like a great, black lake. We got dizzy from
staring, the feeling of looking down instead of up, gravity
reversed, our sleeping bags little canoes of safety.

Still, we kept watch until the curling-rock-shaped ashtray
I'd brought out from the rec room got full. Until the crescent
moon had crossed the sky and Regina grunted, sinking into
dreams, and yanked the dewy sleeping bag to her shoulders.
After the moon went to bed my eyes closed and didn't open
again until the sky had become a bright and stinging blue.

Regina stayed over the next night too, but nothing
happened. We were hanging out in my bedroom the day after
when she said that maybe I'd been tired when I made the
sighting. She lay on my bed, her body all curves and mounds
to my angles and points, her thick, electro-shock hair spread
on the pillow.

'I watched it for half an hour,' I said.

...............................................................

'Okay, Germ. But still, strange things can happen.'

'What things?'

She shrugged. 'Seeing things.'

I rolled my eyes. 'I wasn't *seeing things* in the way you mean. I don't know why it's more likely I'd hallucinate than see a UFO. They've got to exist. And I've never hallucinated before, except –'

'FLASHBACK!' Regina made a crazed face, tongue lolling.

I grinned. 'Yeah, but everything else around me was normal, so I don't think so. And I doubt Mom spiked my dinner.'

'If only,' Regina sighed.

I suggested we make a map. Using one of Ian's astronomy guides, I got Regina to help me copy the July chart onto a big sheet of paper, and then I plotted my sighting. The map looked so good that I decided to make another, of the route to Vancouver. We made a rough sketch of the provinces from Ontario to B.C. and marked Wellington as a happy face with a lobotomy scar in its skull. 'And a zit for Greenview,' Regina said, adding a bright red lump. Then I calculated a per-day mileage and plotted Ian's estimated whereabouts for each night of his trip. Mid-week he'd be in Manitoba. Flipping through the atlas I found a town called Shilo, which sounded close enough to shit, and put a dot there: Ian in his brand-new, stink-free tent.

'He was just hoping to get laid,' Regina said. She gazed thoughtfully at my Jim Morrison poster. 'Ian's got total babe potential. But he has to stop acting like such a freak – just like you.'

'Thanks.'

'Just joking, Germ,' she giggled. She picked up my pencil case and started filling in my route map with drawings, which

..................................................................

she's great at. She added the mountains, plus lakes, swamps, deserts, emblematic animals like salmon and lynx for B.C., and a field mouse in Saskatchewan, the only thing we could think of that might live there. In place of my dots she made cartoons of Ian at each of his stops and had him doing stupid things, like sitting on the kybo.

'Do you think Ian might have seen it?' I asked later, as we trudged up Ferndale Hill Road toward the store, sharing a wrinkled old spliff Regina found in her jeans pocket. I was thinking of that lonely Northern Ontario highway, the outer-space closeness of the night.

'Get real!' Regina coughed. 'Whoa, this tastes like shit.' She took another toke and passed it over, her voice pinched as she held in the smoke. 'From what you said ... that thing ... whatever it was ... was way too close. They wouldn't ... see it in Toronto ... much less ... Wawawa or ...' She exhaled and coughed, thumping her chest with her fist. 'Or whatever-the-fuck up there. They probably didn't even see it downtown. Car.'

'That's a false assumption,' I said, whisking the spliff out of sight. 'We don't know how big it was, so we don't know how far way. Shit, it's dead.' We examined the spliff's remains and agreed to chuck it, our throats raw and parched and not even a buzz. As we walked on I tried to convince her: the UFO could have been enormous, continental – an Antarctica-sized ship flying higher than satellites! If it travelled from another galaxy, even another dimension, then why not? (Regina snickering: 'Whatever, Germaine.') And who knows, maybe it did fly right across Ontario. Skimmed the pine forests and invisible highway, with Ian's campfire the only light point on earth.

* * *

That night Regina lay on her stomach with the flashlight and a novel. 'Tell me if anything happens,' she said with a yawn.

'It was here once, it'll be here again,' I said, craning my neck to the sky. 'We just have to be patient.'

'How do you know? If you saw this place would you come back for more?'

She had a point.

With Ian gone the house was even more boring. No Santana or Zappa pulsing in the rec room (Ian took his stereo, the fucker). No more griping from Dad about the noise, Ian's slobdom and laziness ... no more weekly 'Why doesn't he *do* something, he's so talented' laments from Mom, because he finally was gone to do something: he was off to university to become a physicist. Just like that! A piece of paper and goodbye Greenview, goodbye Wellington, hello great new life.

You can only read or watch TV or escape to friends' places for so long and my parents, off from teaching for the summer, seemed to fill the entire house and both yards. They were gardening, landscaping, cleaning, rearranging, renovating. In the afternoons Frank Sinatra and Tony Bennett trumpeted from the cabinet stereo like the soundtrack to this demented TV series I was trapped in: *Alvie and Cassy and Their House*.

'You're not very talkative,' Mom said at supper. I am *never* talkative (except for arguing with Fart Breath). They just hadn't noticed.

I shrugged and played with my food. Mashed potatoes like mountains. Everything was a joke.

Mom looked sadly at her plate. 'I know someone who needs to cheer up,' she said.

Dad looked at her, then at me. 'Come on, honey,' he said.

'Your food's getting cold.'

I began eating, but only because I was hungry and I hate cold potatoes.

'You don't like sleeping in the house any more?' Mom said after a bit.

'It's cooler out in the tent.'

'Why don't you invite one of your other friends over? You've had Regina a lot.'

'Like who?' I blinked innocently at her. Mom doesn't like any of my friends. She thinks they're all 'smart alecs'.

'What about that Patty girl you used to play with?'

'That was in grade six!'

Mom widened her eyes, pretending surprise. 'Oh, was it? Well ...'

'Well,' Dad said, chewing his beef with gusto, 'Ian should just about be in Calgary by now.'

Swift Current. That's what I'd calculated.

Dad chuckled and squeezed my arm. 'He'll be in sight of the Rockies!'

Christ!

I'd folded my UFO sighting map into a thick square and was carrying it with me wherever I went. I showed it to Jackie and Bono and they laughed but were secretly jealous, I could tell, so to punish them I didn't invite them to spend a night in my tent, even though sooner or later Regina would probably bail, leaving me out there, under the stars, alone.

I had the rec room all to myself now and I lived down there when Regina wasn't around. I could do anything I wanted, anytime. In that one week I read *Chariots of the Gods* and *I, Robot*. I dug to the bottom of Ian's magazine boxes and discovered crinkly copies of *Hustler* and *XXX Couples*, the models with flawless, caramel-coloured skin, even the men's toes. Talk about desperate – actually *keeping* the copies. But I took the couples one and masturbated to it on the rec room sectional. Then I realized that Ian had probably done the same thing and felt really creepy.

I had the rec room's TV all to myself. I watched a dumb movie about a woman who gets impregnated by an alien and becomes obsessed with drinking instant coffee, except no one, not her husband or even the woman herself, knows why – she just seems to be going nuts – until the end when the ship spins down to earth in a blinding dust cloud and snatches her away.

Outside, the endless days of sun baked the neighbourhood deader than usual. Even the birds seemed to have gone. My shoes scuffed up dust as I climbed Ferndale Hill Road. The only people I saw were some kids on bikes, hoovering Popsicles. 'Fall and you'll choke,' I said to one as he whizzed by. He stuck out a purple tongue.

At the variety store I leaned against the hot brick ledge outside. Two little girls in bathing suits with huge beach towels draped over their shoulders trotted by on the sidewalk. They seemed very far away, on another shore across the empty parking lot's haze. I looked up and down the street: deserted. But even a desert's *supposed* to be a desert.

Moms or dads drove up to the store and I stared at them, smoking. They pretended not to notice. *Why don't you get off your fat asses and walk*, I eyeballed as they shot me nervous, damning looks and slid to safety again behind their tinted windshields.

On the way home my scalp got so hot it hurt to touch. Maple saplings were drooping on the boulevards in front of the boxy houses with their silly fake shutters and scalped grass. Everything was so far away: the street wide and empty,

## Clear Blue

............................................................

the harassed lawns vast and useless, and then the houses.
Like nothing wants to touch or be touched. How did we end
up this way? I stopped to light another cigarette and started
crying. *No one really has anything*, the wilted trees seemed to
be saying. *Look! It's all just gunk.* A tear rolled off my chin
and made a dark grey splot on the concrete. I remembered
the thrill of setting up Ian's telescope with him in our yard, a
long time ago, when he wasn't out so much in the evenings.
How it seemed that the moon, just by being there, meant that
something could happen to us. That there was something
important about us. Ian and I would rush into the house for
paper and pencils and laugh at our parents, doped on the TV,
oblivious to what we knew.

Another tear marked the sidewalk. *She left a trail of tears*
... The thought made me smirk, but I still kept crying. The
sun sizzled my head. The air buzzed with invisible cicadas
and lawnmowers as I moved slowly on, but then this faded ...
and warped into the smooth engine hum of alien ships coming
for me: I would be saved from this savage, castaway place –
beamed on board to become their friend. No: they would have
*chosen* me because they knew I was different. I'd go off
exploring the universe for years and years and come back to
Earth still sixteen, though no longer skinny, with flowing hair
and the wisdom of millennia inside me. I'd give databanks of
high-tech information to Ian and he'd become a world-
famous scientist forever in my debt. With my brilliance I'd
show everyone else how fucked up they are. I'd become world
leader. The new Moses. A streak of star-silver in my hair, the
light of far-off galaxies in my eyes.

I knew they'd be back and I was right, though they came just
in time.

Our sixth sweltering night in the rancid pup tent and
Regina was rebelling bad, saying she would only lie around
until midnight and then I had to come out and do something,
I was turning into a goddamn mushroom. After I agreed we'd
go pee on Mr MacIntyre's lawn and then head up to the
variety store, she lay bouncing the flashlight around the yard
and making up a story about perverted things my parents had
secretly buried there. Overhead, the half-seen planets, moons
and suns wheeled slowly forever – and suddenly three of them
moved.

I held my breath. The sky was still. My eyes searched, but
now I couldn't find anything. I pleaded to the UFOs to move
again, to let Regina see. Then I spotted them.

They were round and shiny. Like silver balls in a pinball
machine, and about that size from the ground. Bigger and
much closer than the stars, they were hovering low in the
east. Without taking my eyes from them I touched Regina's
arm, told her where to look.

'But those are just –' she started to say, then groaned, 'Oh
– my – God.'

The UFOs moved. Sped across the sky too fast and wonkily
to be airplanes or weather balloons or satellites. Besides, none
of these travels in packs of three, right? The spaceships did.
Flew in a triangle formation, always together, so we wondered
if maybe they weren't three but one, a vast mother ship with
humongous headlights or reflectors shining from each end,
following the scout I'd seen earlier. Airplanes and satellites
don't hover either, but these (or this) did: circled the Big
Dipper, paused, then cut west, stopped, continued west, then
north toward the highway, then southeast, standing still for as
long as five minutes after each shift, so if you glanced up then
it would be possible not to notice anything unusual unless you

knew your constellations, knew that asteroid-sized formations
don't suddenly appear on steamy July nights.

They were quiet. Moving like points of light.

Regina and I huddled beside the tent and tracked them
with whispers. Saying 'Holy fuck!' a million times. I scribbled
blindly in my notebook, feeling for the page. Time seemed to
stop. Later, I thought of the monkeys at the beginning of
*2001: A Space Odyssey*: small and grunting in surprise.

When they'd gone – zooming west over the rooftops on
Ferndale Hill Road and disappearing as suddenly as they'd
come – we lay on the sleeping bags and took big breaths.
After a while I started to laugh.

'Freak out!' I yelled. 'Fucking freak out of all freakiness!'

Regina convulsed with giggles. I didn't care who woke up.
For the first time in years I felt that there was no place I'd
rather be.

The next day was one of the best of my life, despite the fact
that I hadn't slept at all. I updated my sighting map and on
the back wrote down every detail I could remember. I got
prepared for another UFO stakeout by blowing my allowance
on high-speed film and coaxing Dad to let me use his tripod
and camera. Then Regina called to say that Deirdre, her
mother (who Regina calls by her name – Mom finds this
shocking), had flipped out and ordered her to stay home. Not
because Regina had told her anything, but because Deirdre
was hung up on this principle where five nights at my place
was okay, but six made it almost a week and a week was
*practically a vacation*, an imposition on my parents whether
they minded or not. Then Regina called Deirdre
premenstrual, and that definitely settled it.

We talked about extraterrestrials. What kind of penis

would one have or would there just be nothing, like a store
mannequin? I said, 'They could probably take you back in
time because they're so fast. Where would you go?'

'Why would they do that?' Regina said. She munched
potato chips in my ear. 'They'd cut you open for scientific
experiments. They'd dissect your itty-bitty brain.'

I told her she was making a false assumption. 'You're
acting like people in the movies, thinking that just because
they're aliens, they must be evil.' I was cleaning the camera
lens and it occurred to me that having UFO proof might not be
such a good thing. If the wrong people knew, they would
probably try to blow up the ships without even saying hello
first. That's what I call evil. Or they'd explain them away, say
I was too young and dumb to know what I saw, say the ships
were Russian spy planes and confiscate my photos. UFOs are
just one more thing people don't want anyone to believe. Like
most true or amazing things.

Regina wished me sweet dreams of slimy Martian sex and
told me to call in the morning so she'd know I hadn't been
vaporized.

'For God's sake, that's not going to happen,' I said. I knew
she was joking, but couldn't help feeling pissed off. Killing
and sex: is that all she could talk about? She was so casual
about the sighting too, as if it hadn't changed anything.

Regina gave me her God-from-*The-Ten-Commandments*
voice. 'YES, ASTRO CHILD. ONLY THOU SHALT
REMEMBER –'

I pretended to be already hanging up and pressed the
disconnect.

In the back yard I set up the tripod and spread my
sleeping bag on a ground sheet outside the tent. Though I was
hot, I zipped myself inside. I lay on my back with my hand

inside my tank top, going slowly around my breast. *Orb. I
have orbs.* Maybe that's why I want to be in the sky, I
thought.

After a while Jackie came out onto her deck next door and
called over the fence in her pyjamas. 'Hey German, seen any
little green men?'

I said nothing, which I knew would drive her nuts. She's
another person who'd automatically think the UFO pilots were
evil, unless maybe they looked like fuzzy kittens. Or Mick
Jagger.

I recited songs in my head to stay awake. I lay so still a
cricket hopped onto my forehead, let out a single cheep and
sprang away before I could twitch. Overhead, the stars hung
in their usual places. No orbs shining like pieces of the moon.
No triangular formation flitting and hovering, a cosmic
THEREFORE. Therefore what? But I knew they must be up
there. How far they must have come, through nebulae like
membranes, quadrants, solar systems, years upon years, and
how strange everything here would seem. I took a deep breath
and closed my eyes.

*Talk to me.* I squinted up at the sky. The stars glimmered
down. I shut my eyes again. *Talk to me. I'm here!*

Just before dawn I woke up. I'd slid into the tent and
hadn't been asleep long. Something had happened or was
about to, I knew. My body felt alert. All noise outside had
stopped, air conditioner conked, the pool filter and crickets
dead. I stared up at the tent's peak, where a webby grave of
ancient insects lay invisible in the dark. Then suddenly it
wasn't.

Two curled-up spider husks dangled in a greenish light.
The moon, I thought, it's the moon come out from the clouds.
Or a porch light next door. But the light moved. Trawled the

roof of the tent, paused, then slid away, going west. In the distance was the whine of a truck gearing up on Arbor Lake Road, leaving the city. An echo fading to silence.

I slept outside well into August, but saw nothing. I made a copy of my sighting map and mailed it to Vancouver. The one of Ian's route I shoved in a box in my closet. His letter came a few weeks ago, written to my parents but with a section for me. He said that my map was excellent and that he wishes he could have been there. When I make it to B.C., he says, he'll take me to an observatory. 'What map's he talking about?' my parents asked me, but I just made up something ridiculous.

Recently, I was walking over to Regina's one Indian summer weekend and kept looking up at the cloudless, empty sky. I realized the phrase 'clear blue' didn't work any more. The blue's just the horizon, the edge. Ian is in Vancouver, and those mountains are there though I can't see them. They're soaring in the sky, older than our puny memories, and stronger. They're saying something to each other, and maybe to us, speaking in some language I want to know more than anything on earth.

# Heirlooms

She's got eyes that push into you and I can't believe I once
used to stay with her.

'Oh God, well don't tell her anything this time,' Regina says
when I phone her to complain about the trip to Grandma Scott's.
In the background the Demics are playing, who through some
incredible and joyous error recently performed at our school,
screeching and spitting at the tiny cheering audience.

*I wanna go to New York City, 'cause they tell me it's the
place to be, yeah –*

'I never tell anyone anything,' I say.

'Well, you shouldn't even *talk* to her. Just grunt. She
already thinks you're a savage.'

Back in grade eight, I mentioned to Gram that I often met
friends after school at the variety store. At dinner she snitched
to my parents that I was 'running all over town like a wild
Indian'. Mom's explaination that the variety store was right
across from the school yard didn't help. Next time Grandma
Scott visited and we were alone, she wagged her quivering
turkey neck at me. 'Your mother's nose is plugged,' she said.
'I may be old, but I can still smell trouble. And you, young
lady, are headed straight for it.'

'It looks like the monolith from *2001*.'

................................................................

It doesn't really, but I like to say this. I think it'll bug
Mom, who's so gung-ho on Canadiana.

'Well, I can't imagine people stop often,' she says sadly, as
if the monument gets lonely. I twist in the cramped seat and
watch the black hump shrink and vanish around the bend,
the third or fourth one we've passed along this strip. Battle of
the Longwoods, Moraviantown Site, Tecumseh's Last Stand –
it's like driving through a cemetery.

Mom feels in her purse for sunglasses and I glimpse the
little drugstore bottle of 'nerve pills' in the side pocket, ready.
When she slides on her shades the road flickers in the dark
plastic, a reel of film endlessly spinning. 'We can stop at some
of the monuments on the way back if you want,' she says.

'Maybe.'

'Maybe *what?*' I'm supposed to talk in full sentences.

'Maybe sure. Okay. We'll stop.' I have an essay on the War
of 1812 due Monday. Mom's a teacher (like Dad, like Grandma
Scott was – I'm fucking surrounded), and she's thrilled I'm
doing the war because kids these days don't know anything
historical unless it's on television. She also can't help slipping
me useful info. I write in my notebook: *Moraviantown on the
Thames River: monument like a tree stump. Fields otherwise.
General Proctor and Tecumseh's last stand. Proctor's
disgrace. Mom says Uncle Matt found some old brass buttons
here as a kid.*

I stare at the page. Since leaving this morning I've felt
stunned, like my real body's back home, or not even there.
I've felt like this a lot lately. Being out of town and bumping
along this back-road route make me fuzzy at the edges,
blurred. Here I am doing homework, for God's sake – and
with my mother! Visiting Grandma Scott. Just like old times.

Fields roll past the window, black and watery brown. We

could be looking at an old photograph. Huge open spaces
sprawl between the weathered barns and brick houses. So
much freedom. At home, everything is fences and streets and
driveways, there's barely an inch someone doesn't know
about. Take your bike on a lawn and you'll see: people go
apeshit over their yards, though they never use them.

'I have to go,' I say.

Mom looks worried. 'Now?'

'Sorry.' I don't really need to, but this car ride's going to be
the highlight of my day, so I'd better prolong it.

Mom sighs. 'We'll have to stop in Thamesville.' We're
already running late and Grandma Scott freaks at lateness
(which is strange, because Mom always leaves late when she
visits, and then gets hysterical about time). Still, she doesn't
bite my head off for needing to stop. There are definite
advantages to parents believing you've finally joined their
side.

I'm not partying much these days. After school I come home
and read in the rec room, flake in front of the tube, scribble in
my journal, phone friends. I've even started playing the piano
again, though they'll never rope me back into lessons. Friday
and Saturday nights are the worst: days in advance I map out
what's on TV, as if that could distract me from imagining all
the good times I'm missing – which Regina phones to tell me
about the next day. Saturday afternoons I tag along on
shopping and errand expeditions with Mom because I need to
go somewhere, even if it's hell. We visit the mall. The
supermarket. The public library. Mom buys me nutritious
lunches in food courts. She's never been so happy: she
chatters and chirps as we perk around in her little car with
my long legs folded against the dash like an insect, and once

she even tried to link arms with me downtown. I scuff along
in a daze, unable to believe that this is me. That boredom can
do this to me.

Desperation's a scary thing. Only three weeks have passed
since I got grounded until the end of term (three weeks
without booze or dope!), and it's only October. I still feel the
undercover store-security man's vice grip on my arm, hauling
me back as I headed out the drug store carousel into the mall.
Why me? All I had was a stupid lipstick, and meanwhile
Regina was home free inside the washrooms, her pockets
loaded with cosmetics and cassettes and even an electric leg
shaver. Mom and Dad weeping and raging like I'd committed
high treason. 'We just don't understand,' Mom lamented.
'Ever since you started high school, you've become so
*negative.*'

I grinned. 'It's called getting older.' I was sitting in one of
the plush 'guest' armchairs while my parents stood, just like
the security man had when he'd taken me down to the store's
basement to call the cops. Being sixteen meant no charges,
but a constable had driven me home and talked to Mom and
Dad in the living room, his squad car parked outside for all to
see.

Dad turned so red I thought he'd have to be medicated.
His lips tightened until they vanished. 'Well stealing certainly
isn't part of getting older!' he blurted. 'So you can cut the
attitude. For God's sake, we can't believe you didn't know
better. We're really disappointed in you, Germaine.' Then he
shook his head, sorrowfully repeating, 'Really disappointed,
really disappointed....' All this over a dinky little lipstick!
They've no clue what being bad *really* means, what awful
things I could be doing, the stories I've heard about other
kids. But by far the worst things are done by parents. Mom

and Dad don't know. Their house is their bubble.

In Mom's night table I found a book called *Tough Love: Your Teenager's Secret Need*, which outlines a program of slavery and torture tactics like extended grounding and the refusal of the phone and other 'privileges' until the kid snaps into shape – the shape of a parent clone, of course. If the program fails, the author recommends the last chapter, called 'Loving Disownment.' I was tempted to write over it: *I Didn't Ask To Be Born.*

I still have my privileges. I just don't have a life. Only three weeks, and already I'm Mom's best pal.

'Hi Mom!' Mom squeals like some sorority case and opens her arms to Grandma Scott, who's standing at the end of her front walk in the chilly breeze, a fault-line crease between her eyes. We spotted her as soon as we turned onto the street: a greystone figure under the overcast sky.

In my memory, Grandma Scott's a stale powder puff, a musty drawer. But in person she's huge. Her sturdy legs are set apart. She seems to look down on the car from some windy bluff. My height comes from Grandma Scott, though I didn't get the flesh. Mom's a runt by comparison, a hospital mistake.

Grandma Scott doesn't budge while Mom hugs her, though her dress ripples – not the usual tailored number, but a plain housedress for moving, with orangey nylons withering at the knees. My hello gets barely a nod, but her dark eyes flick over my tight jeans, high-top runners and hair, which I've made big and bouncy with the curling iron. And to think that right now I could have been home, curled up in the rec room by the fake-fireplace heater and listening to some mellow tunes on my crappy record player. Only the thought of losing a privilege keeps me from giving the old bat the finger and dashing back to the car. Instead I go up and kiss her squishy-soft cheek. She smells of dried flowers.

Two sweaty men are already carrying things to a moving van parked in the drive. 'Oh dear,' Grandma Scott says. She pats her short, freshly clipped hair, her habit when annoyed. I follow her gaze to the street, then look quickly away. In the middle, the Morton kids are watching the scene from their bikes. The Morton kids. All six of them.

'Shall we go inside, Mom?' Mom asks in the ridiculous sing-songy voice she uses only with her mother and babies and when she's tipsy.

Grandma Scott's eyes shift from the kids to the truck to my jeans. 'Yes, all right,' she says. It sounds like a warning.

Except for tea things the kitchen's bare. Its bright windows blind me after the foyer's dark wood. Through floating panes of orange and yellow Grandma Scott hands us our cups. Mom keeps her purse on her shoulder.

'Well, it sure looks like you've got it all organized,' she says. Gram claims her arthritis is forcing her to move, and we've been conscripted to help pack. Yet I see little for us to do: the house has been scrubbed down and is cluttered with cardboard boxes marked in Gram's large, clear writing with the words FRAGILE! and THIS WAY UP. She leans against the counter and crosses her arms, her breasts shifting like water balloons until they find new bulges to settle into. She tells us she's exhausted, just exhausted. The impression is that this could have been prevented.

'Do you want me to go and do anything?' I ask.

'Just drink your tea,' she says, 'before it's stone cold.'

Mom opens her mouth, shuts it again.

\* \* \*

## Heirlooms

........................................................................

Grandma Scott has a good side and a bad side. When I was a kid I spent a month every summer with her while my parents went on vacation and my brother got sent to camp. Grandma Scott would always be excited when I arrived. There'd be special meals and outings to the cinema and public pool. She'd teach me how to bake treats we'd eat before dinner, blueberry scones and lemon tarts. We'd stay up late (she never cared when I went to bed) and watch black-and-white movies, and she'd gossip to me about the stars like they were her own neighbours: the plane crash that killed Leslie Howard, Clark Gable's divorces and Mickey Rooney's wives, Jean Harlow living the high life and Judy 'Dorothy' Garland ending up a drug-addict nutcase, poor girl, though she certainly was pretty. Most mornings we walked the few blocks downtown to do errands, and Grandma Scott would say 'Now you hold your head high and don't be shy with strangers, Germaine. You're a Scott, my dear (I wasn't, technically, but this didn't seem to matter), and you have nothing to be ashamed of, by God!' I wasn't sure what I *could* be ashamed of – I hadn't thought of this before – but I smiled the way I thought Grandma Scott would like whenever we met one of her friends downtown, ladies in hats and pearls and buckled shoes like Grandma Scott, men in suits capped with fedoras, everyone always dressed like they just came from church. And often these people would say I was a pretty girl (which no one at home said), though I was awfully pale and thin (which everyone did). Then they'd give me a dime. A pretty good deal, I thought.

Sooner or later the bad mood would come. Rushing into the kitchen in the morning, I'd find Grandma Scott red-eyed, shaking her head. 'I worked so hard all my life,' she'd say, sniffing, 'and look!'

I did look, but everything seemed the same as the day
before. I saw the sunny kitchen with its bottomless cookie jar,
saw Grandma Scott's furniture, antiques like the inkwell and
fountain pen set and the brass fog horn, all so interesting
compared to things at home. But Grandma Scott saw
something else. She'd glare at the twisted-wood chairs and
china figurines like all this was against her. When I said
nothing, she'd include me.

She would start to get dressed in the morning then sigh
'Oh what's the point!' and clomp around the house all
afternoon in her heels, her dress still unzipped past her girdle.
Sometimes she wore no dress.

The wrinkles on her face deepened, like fresh cuts. She'd
say, 'I hope your mother's happy!' If I croaked, 'She is,
Gram,' she'd laugh. 'Well, good! Good for her!' Her smile was
merry but her eyes stayed cold. 'And your father is too, I
suppose,' she'd say with a chuckle. '*He's* always been proud
of himself!' Why was she so mad at my parents? Worry about
this hung over my days. Our family seemed tainted in some
way only Grandma Scott knew. She didn't take me downtown
any more. I wandered around in the vast corner-lot yard
picking weeds and whipping them against the brick, or I
explored the sleepy streets nearby, afraid of going further and
getting lost. I wished my parents would come for me early,
but when I thought of them they seemed changed: they were
people with secrets, people who'd done things.

In her bedroom Grandma Scott has two wooden dressers
for clothes, a wide one with a mirror and a plainer tall one.
The tall one has a key-locked bottom drawer. On top,
Grandpa Scott stares at you from a frame, a serious young
man in uniform. I never knew him. He died in the war way
before I was born, and all I know about him comes from

# Heirlooms

.......................................................................

Mom, who only knew him until she was seven. Since he died Grandma Scott's refused to speak about Grandpa except as a kind of reference point in her life, as in 'That was before I lost my husband' or 'That was after Edward passed away.' Except he didn't 'pass away' – this much everyone knows. He stepped on a land mine in Sicily and got blown to smithereens.

One night I heard her calling me. I slid out of bed and groped down the long hallway toward the horizon of light beneath her door. Inside, Grandma Scott was standing by her bed in a white nightgown and cardigan. The room's only light came from the night table's lamp, which Grandma Scott blocked with her body so the bulb shone through her gown from behind, showing me her long thick legs and the shadowy spot between them.

'See this drawer?' She pointed to the locked one.

'Yes, Gram.'

'I never open this drawer.'

I thought that she was going to accuse me of tampering with it, and panicked.

But Grandma Scott just stared at the drawer. After a while she turned to me. Her eyes were moist, larger in the dimness. She said, 'I've never opened this drawer since my husband died. And I never will.'

I nodded. Somehow I knew that Grandma Scott hadn't told anyone else about this, just like she'd never sob at the table in front of my parents. My insides felt all crumbly and sore, like I was a shape filled with uneven pieces.

Outside, the wind began to spatter rain against the open windows. Drops flew in and made marks on the bedspread, but Grandma Scott continued to look at the drawer. It seemed terribly alive now: a pulsing, slumbering thing made of

Grandpa Scott's remains, singed skin and busted-up bones,
clumps of burnt hair, and a voice that would rip you apart if
it ever got out. Grandma Scott stood with her head bowed for
a long time, as if listening.

She's looking at me over her teacup. 'And how are things at
school?' she asks.

Mom fidgets. I blink. 'Oh fine. Everything's fine.' Truth
from my perspective, a load of bull from my parents'. I
haven't had an A (or many B's) since first-term grade nine,
over two years ago. This fact was harped on again and again
the endless evening the Tough Love regimen was imposed.

'Germaine's writing a paper on General Proctor,' Mom says
brightly.

Grandma Scott's eyebrows arch. Our ancestors were
United Empire Loyalists. 'Well, he was a good man,' she says,
and taps her skull. 'Though a bit slow in the strategy
department.'

I claim the need to use the bathroom (Mom gives me a
look) and slip away. On the can, I take out my cigarettes and slide
one under my nose, hold it unlit in my mouth. The weed smells
gorgeous, like my friends and our places. A whiff of freedom.

I sit as long as I dare, then take the indirect route back. In
the living room, the furniture's all piled at one end like the
house got tossed in a storm. Out in the driveway the movers
are grimacing with Grandma Scott's roll-top desk as they
carry it up the ramp to the truck. The Morton kids are still
watching from the street like it's a TV show. The oldest girl,
straddling a ten-speed with tattered masking tape on the
handlebars, is the only one I know. Jessie. We're the same age.
She looks different now, except for the long black ponytail,
which I remember. I notice her breasts pushing against her

# Heirlooms

................................................................

T-shirt, the pink lip gloss against her dark skin. Her brothers
and sisters go down in age all the way to a chubby toddler in
overalls sitting in a red wagon attached to one of the bikes.
It's weird to see a whole family hanging out together. Where
are Jessie's own girlfriends? But maybe that's how it is in a
small town, and anyway, she seems okay with it. She gets off
her bike to help a brother with his Big Wheel, which has leaves
stuck in it. Two girls call to her like she's their mother, *Look
at me, Jessie, look at me!* as they ride around in circles no-
handed. Suddenly Jessie spots me at the window. Our eyes
click. And here I am, staring outside just like the old piss pot
herself. I should just smile and wave, I really should, but instead I
step back. I can't handle being seen, being *associated*.

Grandma Scott's been fighting with the Mortons as long as
I can remember. I'm not sure how much of what she says
about them is true – not because she's demented, but because
she gets offended by almost everything. So it's not hard to
imagine her hating the Mortons even if they never did
anything, which in itself would be reason to hate them, for
not being neighbourly.

'They prey on me because I'm alone,' she'll say, as if
anyone could take advantage of Gram, who raised three kids
alone and stands almost six feet tall, her arms as big as my
thighs. The 'preying' refers to the few times the Mortons came
over and asked to borrow things, like the lawnmower, or the
infamous time they asked to borrow her car. It also seems to
refer to 'looks' she gets, from Mrs Morton in particular.
Grandma says the woman lounges around all day in cut-off
jeans with patches on the behind and is probably a drinker.
'Not that she can really help it,' she'll add. 'Her people aren't
raised like you.'

\* \* \*

...........................................................................

A fancy wooden case has appeared on the kitchen countertop when I return.

Grandma Scott presents it to me. 'I'm giving you the Scott spoons, Germaine,' she says. The box is opened by a tiny silver latch and has blue velvet lining. The shiny tea spoons lie in slots. They still look new.

'I've given both my girls something,' she explains, 'so you should have the spoons.'

Mom stands at my shoulder. 'They're lovely, aren't they sweetie?'

'Yes.'

Silver spoons for afternoon parties with ladies. Wives. Oh God.

I can't smile. I thank her without looking up, as if entranced by the case's beauty.

Grandma Scott pats my arm like she used to when she was happy. How easy it is to make them like you: just be that clone.

'Now you put those away for when you're older,' she says, suddenly beaming. 'That's a good girl.'

For a moment, all the knots in the room have dissolved. Mom and Grandma Scott grin at one other. Even my face wants to, because it would feel so much better. *A good girl.* Seems like no one's told me that for years. Tears come to my eyes. I turn and slip the spoons into my bag. *That's a good girl.* Yet it's not true, because I don't want to use the fucking spoons, be that nice wife or daughter. And because I don't they'll never stop fighting and punishing and hating me – though they'll call it love.

Mom and I go around wrapping items for the auction house in sheets of bubbled plastic. The house looks completely

different without all its pictures and knick-knacks. For the
first time I see it as something separate from Grandma Scott,
a thing that existed before she arrived, that will go on living
with another family inside after she's dead. 'It'll be so odd,
never coming here again,' Mom says through sniffles. 'It's
where I grew up.' Itchy for a smoke, I pick at a roll of packing
tape, imagining the pure joy I'd feel leaving our house in the
suburbs forever. Echoing around us is the noise of the movers
grunting, calling out instructions in French to each other.
Ugly grey runners cover the hardwood floors. Each time the
men leave the house gets hollower, its insides scooped out like
the meat from a shell. A tangy smell fills the air.

Mom and I take a mirror we've wrapped downstairs.
'Where would you like this?' she asks.

Grandma Scott stands rigid in the dull living-room-
window light. 'Darn those kids,' she mutters.

I don't remember the Mortons not living across the street, but
Grandma Scott always talks about the neighbourhood being a
fair sight better then, when it was just old Mr Morton, 'a fine
man, unlike his son.' It's not because young Mr Morton
married an Ojibwa woman, she says. That would be fine if
they were decent people. There's an Indian couple on the
other side of town who have a lovely home with a rose garden
in the front. I don't think Grandma Scott's ever actually
spoken to Mrs Morton and neither have I, just seen her
stepping out to get the paper. Other than the long black hair
tied in a braid she looked like anyone else with a tan. I did
meet Mr Morton once, though. He told me to come back
whenever I wanted. But I never did.

I was playing outside during an extra bad Grandma Scott
mood. Two days and she'd eaten nothing but ginger-snap

.........................................................

cookies with aspirin and pots and pots of tea, hunched at the
kitchen table. 'Don't you feel well, Gram?' I'd asked, and
she'd looked at the wall wearily, as if my voice came from
there. 'I've been feeling ill for forty years,' she said. I didn't
ask why, I just got the hell away. For the first time ever, Jessie
was out in front of her house alone, skipping on the sidewalk.
We ended up playing together, going into her back yard for
most of the day, where Mr Morton was working in a huge
vegetable garden. He pulled out cucumbers and tomatoes and
made us sandwiches for lunch. I remember thinking he was a
hippie because of his ragged cut-offs and tie-dyed T-shirt.
Jessie teased him and made me laugh at his pale, veiny legs.
'Hey, slug!' she called. 'That's me!' he'd answer.

'Thanks for coming over,' they said, grinning when I
finally left, and I promised to visit again. But the next few
days it rained and then I went home, and by next summer it
seemed so long ago and I couldn't believe they'd still want to
see me, since the famous car fiasco had happened that winter.

'Asking to borrow my car! The nerve!'

This is Grandma Scott's favourite Morton story. She tells it
even more than the one about how she got the town reeve to
serve the Mortons a notice saying they had to cut their lawn.

'And during the worst storm in ten years!'

'What did they want it for?' I asked this when I was older,
just before I stopped visiting Grandma Scott for good. I was
getting fed up with her crankiness, the way even in her good
moods all she did was gossip about what was wrong with
everybody.

'For?' Grandma Scott stopped her dough rolling and
looked across the table.

'I mean the car.' I tried to sound innocent. 'How come they
wanted to borrow it?' I'd realized that she never said why,

just made the request sound like some outrage out of the blue. Grandma Scott glared at me for a long moment. Like I was one of them.

'No reason,' she said finally, waving the question away with her hand. 'Something about Mrs Morton's mother. Nothing *important*.' She banged the pin down and started spreading the dough at high speed. When it was smooth she sat back and breathed heavily. Her eyes searched the room like she wished there was someone else to talk to instead of this lippy girl.

Shaking her head, she began to cut the cookies herself, though that was always my job. 'Tsk,' she muttered, punching out hearts and people shapes. 'Not having the sense to own a car and asking to borrow mine. They didn't even think what might happen to me, left alone here with that storm raging. They didn't even think!'

Mom and I are wrapping a picture in one of the bedrooms when a terrible shriek cuts through the house. For a second we just look at each other, and Mom's face has the same expression as mine: *I can't deal with this*. Then we rush downstairs. Heart attack, I think. Stroke. Mom in a hysterical state and me having to cope. Or maybe a funeral then, tears and mourning erasing all Tough Love measures, setting me free two months early and no more Grandma Scott, ding-dong the witch is dead. But mostly, mostly, as we hit the foyer and burst outside, I'm afraid of a scene. I can't handle a scene.

On the cement walkway leading from the house is Grandma Scott's tall dresser. Grandma Scott's in front of it with her hands to her face, crying out in an awful voice pitched much higher than I've ever heard it go, almost a

squeal. There seem to be many people around: one of the
mover men on his knees trying to gather up a pile of papers
spilled from the dresser's jutting bottom drawer, the other
man hovering next to Grandma Scott but with his head
strangely angled away, like he's afraid of being struck.
Beyond them is a crowd of faces on the sidewalk: the Morton
kids, mouths gaping.

'It's okay, madame,' the hovering man's saying. He raises
his hands near her shoulders and pats the air. Gram won't
shut up. 'It's okay, madame,' the man repeats, looking wide-
eyed at us. 'See? Everything is okay. Nothing is broken.'

But she doesn't see. Grandma Scott's neck veins bulge.
Tears shine on her cheeks. She reaches out with curled fingers
like she wants to throttle the man on the ground, undo the
mess that's scattered at her feet, the drawer burst open in the
knock-about on the stairs, or maybe just from decades of
rust.

'Clumsy brute!' she yells. 'Clean it up! Clean it the hell
up!'

The man's trying, but he's nervous and slow. I feel sorry
for him on his knees, with his jeans slipped down and his
T-shirt rucked, showing the tender white skin above his bum.
Papers have already caught on the breeze and are tumbling
about the yard, sticking in bushes. I dash after them, with
Grandma Scott still cursing and yelling. Her voice gets into
my guts and twists. *Shut up you old bag!* I get split-second
glimpses of the writing in my hands. 'Commended,' I read.
'Train.' Her voice continues – *shut up!* – as I leap on papers
to catch them, trying to go faster. Flashes of company headers
in bright colours, ink writing 'Dear Alice.' Sheets scattering to
freedom.

'Mom, calm down! It's all right!'

# Heirlooms

...........................................................

'Forty years ... forty years ... oh God, oh dear *God* ...'

'No trouble madame.'

Sheets rise end over end and flutter away from my hands. Sweat on my forehead. Grandma Scott's voice is a hot point buzzing in my brain. Years and years of paper whirling, the man who was on his knees running around with me. And a few feet away the Morton kids continue to watch this insanity. Don't they know it's rude? Haven't they been taught?

We bring everything back, breathing hard. The man smooths the papers into the drawer. Some have grey sneaker prints on them.

Grandma Scott seems older: her mouth's a slack line, shoulders drooped. She pats her hair. 'Oh dear,' she gulps as the man who'd helped me tamps the papers then inches the stiff drawer shut. His partner speaks rapidly in French. It's all unbearable: the voices, the watching eyes, this ruckus over a fucking drawerful of paper. The man on his knees checks the ground one last time. *Hurry up!* I follow his gaze and whisper a curse as we spot it together: a man's gold watch lying on the cement. Wristband gone, just a splintered face. Grandma Scott groans hugely, like it's a knife in her gut.

The man doesn't know if he should put the watch away or give it to one of us. When he holds it out to Grandma Scott she shrinks back, covering her face with her hands. How could I have ever stood in her room, with her nightgown gone transparent and her eyes so starved and staring?

'Give it to me,' I say.

I snatch the watch from the man's palm and shove it deep in my pocket so they can all shut the hell up – Mom, the men, Grandma Scott, and the fucking drawer. I glance over at the Morton kids and it's exactly the wrong moment: they're still gawking, slouched on their bikes like they have been all morning, like they have no fucking lives, and just as I look Jessie leans over her handlebars and whispers to one of her sisters, a girl with an orange stain ringing her mouth. I hate that stain. Jessie slides her eyes to Gram, clearly talking about us. She and her sister look at each other and giggle.

I can't take it.

I don't know why, but I suddenly do something I haven't since I was a kid: I flip out. Anger whizzes through me like in those cartoons where the thermometer in the sick person's mouth shoots red up the glass and bursts the top. I step toward Jessie and shout 'Get out!'

She looks up, shocked.

'You heard me, get out! Go on!' I lunge towards them. I feel airy and wild, paper tossed on the wind. Something's pushing me on.

The younger kids scramble to turn their bikes around. Far away I hear Mom calling my name. 'This isn't a goddamn circus!' I yell and the kids retreat as if blown back, pedalling hard across the road. All except Jessie, who's only moved her ten-speed off the sidewalk. Her dark eyes shine coldly, unafraid.

'I wasn't doing anything,' she says.

'You're sitting there laughing.'

'So? It's funny.' She smirks.

I step toward her. 'You don't know anything. You're just a stupid squaw –'

I stop as if shot. Jessie's bottom lip trembles. My last word rings in the air and I gulp, trying to swallow it back down my throat like stinging puke. How could I have said that? I've never used that word, I've never even *met* another Indian before.

Jessie leans over and in one quick motion spits on the

ground by my feet, then angles her bike away.

I watch her go. The hot wind that inflated me dies. The blood drops from my face right down to my feet, like it's trying to run away. I want to run away too, from this me-thing that's not me. *Don't*, I want to call out. *Don't hate me.* Jessie rides up her gravel driveway, dumps her bike and dashes into the back yard. By the hasty way she does this I know she's crying. I close my eyes. *Please don't cry.* The wetness comes. *It's not what you think because it's not me. This isn't the real me!*

The car engine drones, field after flat field. I keep my face turned to the window. My forehead hurts like hell and I've asked Mom for aspirin and then for a nerve pill, which she refused. I keep touching my fingers to the cold glass then pressing them to my face like a cloth. After a long time of silence, Mom asks how I'm feeling.

'Hungry.'

This starts her off. 'I don't know what you were doing, yelling at that girl like that. What terrible language! God, between you and Mom, what a day!' We spent the afternoon nursing Grandma Scott until my aunt arrived, directing the movers and reassuring them over and over that it wasn't their fault and no one would call to complain. Mom shakes her head and sniffs, but she's pissed-off crying, not sad.

'Lord, you'd think my father was the greatest man on earth, the way she carries on.'

'What was he like?'

'I haven't the slightest idea. And your grandmother wants to keep it that way.'

'Why?'

'Oh goodness knows, Germaine. I gave up asking her years

ago.' She cries for real now, quietly, the tears dropping onto her cheeks, which are starting to show the first long creases of age.

I watch the road. After a while, I lean across and kiss her. 'Sorry, Mom.'

The fields flow past. Since the end of summer, the farmers have been busy. Everywhere the soil's groomed into small, perfectly even waves, grooves and peaks rippling so naturally you'd think it was always this way. Sometimes in the middle of a field there's a big solitary tree that for some reason never got chopped down. The grooves part around it, expertly close to the trunk. In the distance a thin line of trees appears and disappears, appears and disappears, marking the course of the river.

We pull in to the monuments and I copy down the information on the plaques, though it's not much different from what's in my textbook. Each stop's the same thing: car park, garbage bin, a couple of benches, the stubby monument. Only Tecumseh's has a face etched onto the plaque, a man with feathers in his hair.

I'm glad when the stops are over. The rest of the way home I plot how I'm going to sneak out of the house over the next two months. I need to start drinking again as soon as possible.

# The Academic Adviser

**I.**

It was a threat – go or you get four weeks' detention instead of two – and I'm sure Fixler doesn't know what really happened. But back then, last November, I thought Fixler knew everything. About MacKenzie, I mean, not *everything*. I thought all the teachers, custodians, cafeteria and office staff were like feelers, each squint and frown a signal to Fixler's brain. How else to explain the way Fixler can appear where you least expect – strolling through the weedy east parking lot just when you've lit a doob, turning the hall corner as you're calling your friend a sex-starved hosebag. So that's what I thought, what I was thinking, when I first went to see Mr Grearson: it's Fixler, with a different head.

I'd always assumed that the door next to the main office was a utility closet. It has no number and is never left open, but it wasn't locked when I arrived that day as instructed, and inside I found a short corridor with several more doors, these with name plates on them. On one the name said 'Mr A.J.I. Grearson, Academic Adviser'. Wondering about that 'I', I knocked. A voice said to come in and there he was, this brown hulk in the cramped room, sitting as I found he always did, his chair swivelled sideways behind the desk that was totally clean except for a little stand-up calendar, a container of pencils and pens, a glass of ice water, and a lamp that shone yellow light. I don't know where he got the ice.

I sat opposite and he began. He had a fluttery voice that was strange in a large man, like he'd once had a stutter. He turned his head to talk to me but the rest of him stayed at a right angle. Otherwise, it was pretty much like I'd expected. Why was I failing math, why were my other grades so low. Then came the time of being quiet, where I was supposed to be contemplating how serious this was, before he made his decision. As I was waiting he stood up and went to the filing cabinet, and I saw that he was even bigger than he looked behind the desk. His jacket strained against his belly and bunched at the buttons. He wore great boat-sized shoes that sank into the carpet. Clutching a file, my file, he heaved back into his chair. Fixler had a file about me on his desk too, the afternoon he forced me into academic counselling, and as I watched Mr Grearson open the folder and hold it so I couldn't tell what was inside I began to get a headache thinking about these files, these pieces of myself, and how many I've seen lurking on the desks of principals and secretaries, doctors and piano teachers, though I'm only seventeen, and all the ones I haven't yet seen and maybe never will, and when does it ever stop.

For what seemed like ages, the only sound in the room was the turning of paper. Mr Grearson's eyes trailed left to right, left to right. I slouched in my chair and tried to casually yank the crotch of my jeans, which had come out of the dryer that morning (wriggled into and zipped up lying horizontal on my bed) and still felt like they were bisecting me. When Mr Grearson finally closed the file and placed it on his desk he told me I couldn't drop down from Advanced Stream mathematics to General Level like I suggested because my public school grades showed I was obviously very capable in math, therefore mustn't be trying.

'But I'm failing!' I said.

Mr Grearson repeated that this wasn't because I couldn't do the work. Why wasn't I doing the work?

'It's *boring*. I *hate* it.' I sighed and rolled my eyes. I hate the teacher too: Mr Vanderhoven, a loudmouth who calls students by their last names, laughs at his own jokes and loudly sighs at wrong answers. Mr Vanderhoven, who wears white leather shoes and tinted glasses that hide his eyes, who stands at the front of class with his year-round tan, swinging the blackboard pointer like it's a golf club. Mr Vanderhoven, who has grey hairs with bits of stuff in them curling from his ears. Who I once saw dump his dashboard ashtray onto the MacKenzie parking lot before driving off, and whose cigarette butts, when examined by me, had orange lipstick stains on them. Mr Fucking Vanderhoven, who teaches class with a perpetual nipple hard-on under his snug golf shirts and actually accused me, in front of everyone, of chalking an 'obscene symbol' on the board when I scribbled my initials too sloppily beside my algebra solution. I dream constantly of a world where personality and intelligence tests would prevent a person like Vanderhoven from ever getting near a classroom. But I didn't say this to Grearson. I was expecting him to get angry right about now, like Fixler does with 'bad attitude'. Instead, Grearson's lips turned up in a little smile.

He examined the water glass in his hand, rotating his wrist so the ice cubes bobbed and clinked. I wasn't sure what this quiet time was about. He was an older man, easily old enough to be retired. An ex-teacher, probably. Dark skin and large pores on his face. He seemed to be covered in a thin film of oil or sweat, so even his liver-spotted scalp shone a little under the wisps of grey hair, but he leaned back in his chair and gazed into the glass like this was the most comfortable place to be. Minutes passed. He sipped the water. He held it to the lamp's light.

I wondered about his sanity.

Teachers never listen to arguments. That Mr Grearson was actually considering changing his mind about my math class seemed so unlikely that when he finally told me we should talk about this again the following week, I wasn't sure whether to be hopeful or afraid.

## II.

Heading to detention, I spied the thick silver hair and quarterback shoulders of Fixler, making his rounds at the end of the day. I slowed. With steady steps, Fixler advanced down the hall like some silent-but-deadly cleaning machine, eliminating the dirt. Kids dropped their voices as he neared. Locker doors glossy with posters were shut. He paused behind a couple who were kissing and without any words being said they melted away from each other red-faced and vanished in the crowd.

I tried not to look at him as we passed, but couldn't help it. Fixler spotted me and stopped.

'On your way to detention, Germaine?'

This wasn't a real question, like I'd actually answer 'No sir, I'm off to raise a little hell and set a bad example for other students.'

'Yes sir,' I said.

He made one of those grim 'This hurts me more than it hurts you' nods. I smiled and fired my secret Fixler weapon: Fixler's kids. Looking steadily at him, I thought about Fixler's sons, Jimmy and Murray, who went to my public school and

were geeky four-eyed losers then, and who now go to
MacKenzie, where everyone picks on them brutally because of
their asshole ex-football-star dad. And they hate him.

In detention we're supposed to work on something, so I
wrote out song lyrics. Tunes from *The Wall*, which I'd just
seen at the theatre, and songs that I make up. In grade seven I
had a teacher who as punishment for talking in class made us
copy out a hugely long and stupid poem called 'Casey at the
Bat'. Not once, but five or ten times. Evenings in front of the
TV I'd fill half a notebook, and I can't remember one line of it
now.

I told my parents I'd volunteered for the yearbook
committee after school. Mom gushed that it was wonderful I
was 'getting involved' (like my friends are nobody). If she
knew the kind of shiny-toothed ass-lickers who put together
MacKenzie's yearbook – scurrying about snapping photos
during home-game days and charity food drives – Mom
would have been orgasmic.

In detention, I wrote out song lyrics.

## III.

When I saw Mr Grearson for the second time he asked if there
were any improvements to my standing in Mr Vanderhoven's
class. I said it was hard to tell after only a week and he
agreed that this was true, an improvement wouldn't be
immediately noticeable, and after that he stopped asking me
about math at all.

Christ, he was playing with his glass again.

'Should I go now, sir?' I said.

Grearson looked like he'd been startled from a dream.

'Go?' His eyebrows knotted. 'Of course not.' There was a bit
of classroom edge in his voice.

We sat in silence. I looked at the few uninteresting things lying in the dim light. Grearson didn't seem to expect anything. Finally I brought up math again, because I didn't know what the fuck else I was supposed to be doing in his office. He told me he just wanted to wait and see about my dropping down, because as I'd said, a week was hardly much time to assess the situation, right? End of conversation.

I vowed to say nothing more to the loony blob until he did.

From the corridor came the muffled sound of other doors being opened and shut. The band of light under the door flickered and returned. It was a sleepy kind of office, but I didn't feel that way. I was wide awake, waiting for the hook. The whatever-the-hell-this-guy-was-doing to come down.

'So how'd you get the overhead lights turned off?' I blurted when I couldn't stand it any more. I was curious, though, because Grearson's office was the only place in the entire school where the fluorescents were dead. In the classrooms that actually have windows, teachers never flick the lights off, even on the brightest days. Sunshine streaming in becomes a pale yellow glare that's only a little better than the painfully bright electric lights humming softly in your ears all day, making you feel like the air's full of tiny insects trying to work their way into you.

Grearson smiled like he had a secret. 'I have an allergy,' he said. He folded his hands across his paunch, as if pleased to be telling me this.

'An allergy to what?'

'To fluorescent lights.' He glanced at the darkened ceiling. Right – most definitely bonkers. It explained everything.

'I've never heard of that,' I said, trying not to seem doubtful. Like, how would he go around in the building? Eat his lunch? Pee?

'So what happens to you when you're, uh, when the lights are on you?'

'Oh, nothing much.' He waved a hand. 'I just don't feel well after a while.'

I sprang forward in my chair.

'Ha!' I pointed at him. 'Imagine, just *imagine* sitting under them all day like we have to!' I told him about the classrooms then, the anti-sun conspiracy, the buzzing, migraine-inducing tubes. Pompous ass, I thought, hanging out in his quiet little haven here with the calm light, doing fuck all but drinking his water.

Mr Grearson swivelled to face forward for the first time and I braced for an ugly blast. He smiled. 'So you have an allergy to fluorescent lights too, Germaine?' he said.

## IV.

It felt weird, but I went back the next week and the weeks after because he was the Academic Adviser, so I could hardly say no, although at the end of each appointment Grearson would act like it was my choice to come again. 'Same time next week?' he'd say, and I'd nod without meeting his eyes because it didn't feel normal: no secretary to go through, no other students waiting in the corridor. Grearson didn't even check his calendar. And I wasn't getting academic advice. Grearson did ask me once what I planned to do at the end of high school. I said I wanted to move to Paris and work in a bar. 'That sounds fun,' he replied, smiling the little smile that made it impossible to tell whether he was joking or not.

Always the water glass, and sometimes his hands trembled.

He let me get away with things. He asked me to tell him why I hated MacKenzie. I had to say something – not all that I really thought, of course – so I tried different answers. I spent most of one appointment, for instance, talking about the school washrooms. I described the dripping plastic udders of liquid soap that's the colour of pool scum and won't lather, the squares of scratchy stiff toilet paper that don't even fit the containers properly and end up in heaps on the damp floor. Then there's the puke-pink colour of the stalls, the signs that shout NO LOITERING.

'Do you know that our desk chairs are actually made of cardboard? It's coated in this hard stuff, but still breakable. Why do teachers get comfy chairs, when we have to sit much longer than they do? Are their butts more fragile? The answer's obvious: we don't count for anything. In the nineteenth century they put us in factories, now it's schools, which everyone thinks is nicer, but underneath, underneath …' I'd gotten a bit carried away.

Grearson blinked, fingers to his lips. He gave a little nod whenever I hesitated.

I wanted to tell him about the smoking pit, too. How we, the coolest people at MacKenzie, are relegated to this dark overhang with cement benches bumpy with ancient chewing gum and ice cold in winter. How the cafeteria windows along the pit's inside wall let the precious non-smokers and anti-tokers inside watch us like we're inmates in a hoodlum zoo. But I worried that this stuff might lead to other topics – such as what else we do out there. Instead I complained about the desks. The classrooms without windows. The teachers.

I said the word 'damn'. Then 'shit'. Grearson's lips puckered, but that was all.

I said I smoked because it made me feel better. I could have a cigarette in his office, Grearson said, except he didn't have an ashtray. Next visit I brought an empty juice bottle with me and lit up. Smoke filled the room, like we were sitting in some hazy, back-alley café in a land that has such things.

Although I kept going back and watched what I said, I was still totally paranoid that something in our meetings was going to be used against me. At times I refused to say anything. Grearson would try to make me relax. He made dumb jokes.

'Germaine, I can't believe you have nothing to say.'

'Why should I?'

'Well, you're such a good talker!' He chuckled, but it sounded phony, as if he was nervous himself, and as soon as he said these things his cheery face would drop like he regretted them.

My dreams turned worse than usual. People in lab coats performed experiments I couldn't see. But I knew the subject was human, I heard horrible gurgling sounds – and I was next. At school, I kept expecting something bad – a summons to Fixler's office over the PA, though I couldn't imagine what exactly for. What *was* Grearson telling him? Or was he at all? And if he wasn't, if Fixler knew nothing, what would happen when he found out? I knew, I absolutely knew, that any weirdness would be construed as my fault.

Walking to MacKenzie one morning, I gave Jackie a play-by-play of my Grearson visits. She flipped right out. Said the guy was clearly either a pervert, deranged or in cahoots with Fixler to spy on the smoking pit crowd, recording everything in my file for future use.

'But I haven't told him anything incriminating.' It was true. Not even about people I didn't like. Jackie said it didn't matter. I had to stop going.

I laughed. 'If he starts playing with himself behind his desk I'll leave.'

Jackie's always freaked out by weird people. Besides, I had a feeling that she was jealous: I was getting out of my spare to see Grearson, and the guy obviously liked me. Or something. Maybe that's just what I was supposed to think?

## V.

His eyes weren't the eyes of a teacher.

He looked happy, like he'd just come to life, whenever I showed up. It seemed wrong. Maybe it was like Jackie said and the guy just enjoyed my legs? But that didn't seem right either, and Grearson and I had moved the meeting time to coincide with my spare, so it was either sitting in a classroom doing homework I didn't want to do or sitting in Grearson's office, smoking a butt and chatting. He liked puns. Awful puns. 'Has Miss Rowan taught fourth conjugation verbs yet?' he asked once. And then he laid on one of his worst: 'Veni videre video.'

'I suppose that kind of thing's very old-fashioned to you,' he said, after an agonized groan from me. He suggested that I tell him a joke.

'I don't think you'd want to hear any of the ones I know,' I said with a grin.

He picked up his glass and gave the water a swirl. 'Try me.'

Did I know a joke that didn't involve sex, drugs or major swearing? Finally I told a Newfie joke. It was pretty lame. Grearson looked disappointed. We sat quietly again, and then he asked me about math. I'd had a test back and told him my mark.

'That's hardly an improvement.'

I shrugged and said I hated tests.

'When you do badly,' Grearson said. 'You probably

wouldn't if you were doing well. I'll bet you didn't hate tests one bit in public school, when you got straight A's.' He tapped the file, which sat on his desk. My file.

I fidgeted in the chair. What he said was true, but somehow it wasn't the point. And I didn't want to talk about my shitty grades, my not trying and all that.

'Once,' I said, 'in public school – I think I was about nine years old – I had to go for a special test. At least they told us it was a test, and we all had to go, the whole grade, except one at a time. I was one of the last to go. You went outside to one of the portables and you met with this young woman in blue jeans who invited you to sit and play a game with her. I thought this was really strange, because we'd been told it was a test. So I thought, oh, they must be testing the game, seeing how well kids learn it. The woman and I played the game for a while – I don't remember it really, it was just some board game involving numbers – and then she said she was going to give me a gift for my time. That's exactly what she said, "a gift for your time." She left the table and came back and handed me a brown paper roll that felt like coins. Ten dimes, she said. Back then my allowance was a quarter a week, so I was pretty blown away. As I was shoving the roll in my pocket and the woman was resetting the game, she said "You can contribute to the collection on your way out, if you want." She nodded toward the door. What collection? I asked. "Oh, it's just a collection for the kids at the next school we visit, because we may run out of money for gifts and they won't all get the same amount." I went to the door and looked into this Tupperware tub on a table there, half full of dimes.

' "Sure," I said, peeling back the paper on my roll. "I'll give one." And I put a dime into the pile. I thought this was nice of me.' I smiled at Grearson, who I figured probably thought I was only interested in whining and running wild and hadn't a nice bone in my body.

'So I opened the door to leave,' I went on, 'but then I stopped. I was happy about the money, but I still didn't get it, the whole thing seemed wrong. The woman was making tick marks on a sheet of paper. "So, are kids doing well on the game?" I asked. She glanced up. "Oh we don't care about the game," she said. "We just wanted to see how much you'd share. Close the door as you leave, please."

'I stepped outside and shut the door. I stood on the portable's steps. I remember that the sky was very white and hurt my eyes and the wind was blowing hard across the school yard, yet I couldn't breathe, my stomach felt kicked right in. I wanted to run back inside and pour all my money into the bowl, but I knew it wouldn't matter now, would probably not even be allowed now, and besides, I hated that bitch way too much.'

My voice cracked. I was suddenly aware of how I sounded and slouched further in the chair. But I didn't like the silence in Grearson's office either, and shot back up. 'You see? That's why I hate this place.' I swept my arm around the room. '*Teachers.* Right! They're all the same. Assholes. Total fucking assholes. They don't give a shit about anyone but themselves. We're all just some big experiment.' I was standing, now with my hand on the door knob and my bag clutched, mimicking. 'Do our courses. Take our tests. Think our thoughts. Suck our dicks. WELL FUCK EVERYONE!'

Grearson's watery eyes glinted in the lamp light. I thought he was either going to cry or hit me.

'I don't agree,' he said quietly.

I grunted and gave him a smirk. I thought he was full of shit. But then he said something that made me so lightheaded

I felt like I was floating far away from MacKenzie, looking back on it as something very small and old.

He rolled the glass between his palms as he spoke. 'It's true, they're mostly like that, mostly the same. Most people like it that way. But you shouldn't believe they're all the same. No more than every student is the same.'

We looked at each other. His eyes weren't the eyes of a teacher.

## VI.

I freaked. I stopped going.

Jackie had been getting more and more insistent that I tell her what 'happened' in Grearson's office. Her face crinkled in a sneer, she'd made cracks about my 'affair with the guidance counsellor' out on the pit. And she'd also started to not believe what I said. Not that she accused me of lying outright – she'd just insinuate. 'Hmm,' she'd say, when I related the latest meeting. Her lips would purse, like she knew things I didn't.

'You don't believe me?' I asked.

'Give me a light.'

'You don't believe me?'

'I didn't say that.'

'Then what do you mean by "hmm"?'

She carefully blew out the match. 'It's just all very interesting. That's all.' God, she's a bitch!

When I stopped going I told her I was just bored. I'd been going for over two months, Grearson and I didn't have anything more to talk about. I don't think Jackie bought this. Though of course she'd been hoping for some catastrophe, to prove she'd been right.

Weeks went by, the grey winter days lengthening at last,

but instead of feeling better, I was paranoid and guilty. I
bolted the other way if I saw Fixler, convinced Grearson had
handed him my file, thick with notes on everything I'd said. I
felt naked, a glass bowl full of punishable thoughts.
Whenever I had to pass the main office I cowered, yet couldn't
help looking back at the closed, blank door.

Then one day I woke up and wasn't freaked out any more.
I went upstairs on my lunch hour and tried the corridor door.
It was unlocked, but I got no response when I knocked at Mr
Grearson's office. Where could he be? I'd never actually
thought about him being anywhere other than this room,
hidden away like an old trunk in the closet. I waited for a
while, then decided to try the other doors, which had names I
didn't recognize and were offices for people I'd never seen. I
knocked on two of them and got nothing. The last door was
answered by a pretty woman with red hair and blue
eyeshadow, whose face looked worried when she opened up
but turned annoyed when she saw it was me. She didn't know
Mr Grearson's schedule, she said, and told me I should try the
main office. 'Are you an academic adviser?' I asked. I'd
wondered why I never met any other students in the corridor.

'No, I'm not,' she replied slowly, like I was retarded. 'You
need to go to the main office.'

In the main office the old secretary we call Lassie (tufts of
dark hair stick up from the back of her collar) told me Mr
Grearson wasn't in that week and she wasn't taking
appointments for him right now. I should come next week.
When I did, he was still away. The third time I asked, Lassie
told me the exact same thing and I pointed out that I *had*
been coming back like she suggested. She got very huffy then,
clacked her nails on the counter and said there was nothing
she could do.

For the first time I began to wonder what Grearson did when he wasn't at MacKenzie. Where he lived, why he didn't have a wedding ring. What wound had left that peculiar scar on his right hand, running from the base of the palm up around his thumb. I was reminded of my dead grandfather, who was killed in the war. I looked Grearson up in the phone book and found an A.J.I. on a street in Oakdale, a neighbourhood on the other side of downtown.

I tried to make another appointment. As I was at reception Fixler breezed out of his office. My chest tightened.

'Mr Grearson?' he said, slapping his hand on the counter. 'You can't see him.'

My insides felt crushed. I was dust. This had all been wrong, very wrong. A trap. I'd even known it was a trap and fallen in. I was fucked.

'How come?' I asked through the clog in my throat.

Fixler's eyes narrowed. 'What is it that you want to see him about?'

'I've been seeing him … a little.' I coughed. 'About academic advising?' This seemed to do nothing to Fixler. I went on, a little more hopeful.

'You sent me to see him last term, sir, the last time I was up in your office?'

Fixler frowned. He obviously couldn't remember. 'Oh yes,' he said. 'How did that go?'

'Fine thanks.'

'Good. Glad to hear it Germaine. And that we haven't had to see you up here again,' he added, heading back to his office.

I said, 'Oh, but I wanted to make another appointment with him, sir, but Mr Grearson hasn't been in.'

Fixler turned. 'Oh yes.' His lips pressed into a tight line.

....................................................................

'Well. You can't see him, I'm afraid, because he'll not be coming back here. You can make an appointment with another adviser.'

'Not coming back?'

Fixler gave me his 'you're pushing it' look: eyebrows up, eyelids down. He lowered his voice to almost a whisper, as if we were talking about something embarrassing. 'Mr Grearson's very ill. In hospital.' He shook his head and stepped into his office. 'I'm afraid he's not likely to come out again.' The door closed.

I turned to Lassie, who was still at the counter, like she might tell me this wasn't true. Then I left very fast.

I shoved my way downstairs to MacKenzie's front doors. Cold rain pelted my face as I hurried down the steps and the hill, past the bleachers, the running track, far out across the mucky football field under the cloud-heavy sky. *Asshole!* I shouted once I was certain Fixler couldn't hear. *Prick!* I looked back at his office window. It should have been Fixler in that hospital, not Grearson. Mr Grearson, without his suit or his water glass, lying in a strange bed and staring up into those bright hospital lights.

## VII.

He didn't come back. Though who knows, maybe he just retired for real? Once I rode my bike over to the address I found in the phone book. I went at night. A light glowed in the living room, but the curtains were drawn.

I hung around, straddling my bike in the shadow of a hedge across the street. It seemed important that I remember the house, ordinary as it was. I think I knew, then, what's come true now. That Grearson wouldn't really be leaving, not from my head.

I find myself thinking about him in the oddest places. Unloading the dishwasher on Sunday morning while my parents lie in late and the floor creaks overhead. At Jackie's, listening to her latest album and analysing the incredibly obvious affair her mom's now having with a man on the other side of our crescent. Or at last weekend's bush party, when a dumb drunken guy tried to do a 'fire walk' and tripped on his face right in the burning logs. God knows how but only his hand got burned, though that was bad, and he whined and clutched it with his face squeezed tight until someone wet a T-shirt in the river and wrapped it around. His buddies took him away up the path. The guys who'd cheered on the fire walk were still tossing back beer and winging the empties into the woods. One of them called out *Suck.*

And there I was, wondering what Mr Grearson would have said if I'd told him this story. Jackie would say it's ridiculous, thinking about this old man. But in my head, I tell him all the things I never said in his office, that I wish I had. I tell him to see how he takes it, but also so he knows I'm not as stingy as I acted, that I can do more than play games. I just needed to know he wasn't part of it first. I wish Mr Grearson could have told me that first.

........................................................

# Bread and Stones

He said it was the love of God that made me what I am,
except that I am turned away from it. But I don't see how you
can love something you don't believe in, be something you
don't know.

Everything's going great until I head outside to grab more
brew from Daniel's truck at the wrong moment. Or maybe I
just turn my head at the wrong moment, when the denim-
and-leather-jacket crowd hits the right configuration for a
face to flash out at me, a glimpse of fire in the dark. (There is
a fire, actually, roaring in a pit beside a pile of logs at the end
of the drive, but he's nowhere near it.) My fingers, submerged
in half-melted cooler ice, stop moving. There's a little flare
inside my chest, like when your ears pop. Yet even as this is
happening I know that the boy laughing with his buddy really
isn't who I think – for obvious reasons, but also because he's
too tall and looks only vaguely similar. I keep staring, though.
When my hand starts to ache I pull it out, fingers straining
around two bottles of Old Vienna. Tighten the cooler and
slam the back of the truck so the windows shake.
    Squeezing through the kitchen into the living room I find
everyone gone, a group of peroxide girls from Morwood Park
faking boredom in what was our spot by the stereo, their

shadowy eyes flicking across the crowd. I pop a beer. In the dining room a haze hangs thick above the table, where a major bottle-toke session's going down and Regina's on some guy's knee, his face lost behind her freshly permed hair. 'Germ!' she calls when she sees me. I hand her the other beer. Daniel's now gone outside to find me, she thinks.

On the back porch steps I smoke a cigarette and scan the crowd for him. The porch lights spill onto the yard, cast enormous, angular shadows on the shifting bodies, then seem to end abruptly at a wall of darkness – the field's edge. A strange house, this, a farmhouse that isn't any more, stuck alone on flood-plain land with Greenview grown up on the other side of the river. Squinting, I think I can see the blacker shape of trees at the field's far end, in the ravine that slopes to the water. Christopher's face comes to me. I remember the look-alike in the crowd and pick him out from the shadows again. But he really isn't much like Christopher except for the bones, that same pointy chin, that long white neck. Suddenly, I want more than anything to be alone. I do another quick check for Daniel, then step onto the ground. I think I'm heading off to the old barn, but I find myself gravitating in another direction, toward the imposter with the pale skin.

Christopher Weir. I met him downtown just over a year ago, one early Saturday morning in April when I was hungover as hell. He looked like he'd never had a drink in his life. I was in the lineup at Music World to get a free copy of the new Stones album and enter a draw for concert tickets. Stores weren't even open yet. A wormy smell on Main Street, tires swooshing. Early-morning downtown people with their noses sunk in take-out coffee cups. A man with dirt in the lines of his face and pant legs tangled in the zippers of his galoshes stopped to ask what was going on and didn't understand the answer. *Stones? Why the hell people want stones?!*

I was sitting on a plastic bag on the ground, in a forest of mud-splashed denim and Adidas. Jeff 'the Pig' Jackson's party had been the night before, and I was trying to settle the memories in my head – to get rid of them, actually. I'd had about four hours' sleep, I may have still been a bit drunk (sometimes it's hard to tell), and I first noticed him among the other passersby because he was cute and had a black Lab that had grabbed what looked like a pop can in her jaws. The two of them were tussling over it on the sidewalk, and at one point he noticed I was watching, and smiled. Then the line was stirring and I stood, swallowed a mouthful of saliva and blinked in the spit of rain. I CAN'T GET NO, someone up ahead started singing. Baseball caps and limp hair edging toward the Music World marquee.

He came over. Talk about smooth, I thought, but soon realized I was wrong, he had no idea of smooth. He was just *nice*. Cool enough looking – his clothes, I mean, though he was wearing a scruffy old football jacket too short in the arms, its school crest torn off. He wasn't very interested in the giveaway and we only spoke for a moment, a nothing-special conversation while his dog sniffed my shoes. But it was one of those odd situations. In between sentences we kept staring at each other and it was tense, because we were strangers, but also easy, like we were already friends. I don't remember ever having a fantasy about a tall boy with reddish-brown hair and a bony face, but I felt suddenly like I'd been having one for a long time, and here he was.

Coming out of Music World with my album tucked under my arm I tried not to hope he'd be waiting, yet he was right there, leaning against a parking meter, reading. He slapped the book shut and grinned. The Lab thumped her tail against the sidewalk, then leapt up and drove her nose into my crotch.

'Gal!' he gasped, his face terrified and then cracking up when he saw mine. Both of us flushed and giggling, almost staggering with the embarrassment – a hit of adrenaline, an instant high. Yet the second we started to walk together, I realized my mistake. That black leather spine. That fake gold lettering. A Bible. Dream boy was reading the fucking Bible.

Jesus freaks and nerds for Christ. Christians don't drink or swear. They don't have sex before marriage. They dress badly. They think pot is evil. And good music, of course, unless it's by 'Christian rock' bands who should be shot for using the name. At school there's a contingent of flood-wearing God lovers, little factories of dandruff and God-okayed swear words, drat, oh gosh, my goodness. Get fucking real.

But Christopher Weir was beautiful. Deep red lips against creamy skin, and that thick hair I already wanted to get my hands in. Walking beside me with a long-limbed stride.

He didn't want to tell me anything about his school, which I knew meant weirdness – the jacket's missing crest. 'It's religious, right?' I said.

He grinned like he'd expected the question, and looked at the sidewalk. 'If I said yes, would you hate me already?'

We didn't listen to the same music or go to the same movies, but it turned out we read some of the same books. Wyndham, Tolkien, Herbert, Orwell. 'So what do you think of *The Chrysalids*?' What do you think, what do you like? he kept wanting to know. We walked all the way down Main, past the shopping area, the strip of used record stores and pinball arcades full of dealers and narcs. Past the all-night

coffee shops and diners built into old houses, the steepled
church, the empty lots and wire fences thick with snagged
candy wrappers and disposable drink cups, which made Gal
tug on her leash. We walked all the way to the corner of Brant
Street, where I catch the bus north to Greenview. I've never
had such a long conversation about books with anyone, not
even my brother, who's given me almost everything I've read.

'You're from the north end?' Christopher laughed. 'I
thought only assholes lived out there.' He was just teasing,
getting me back for smirking at his musical taste (AM radio
and Bob Dylan's conversion albums – barf!). But I was still
annoyed.

'At least I don't carry around a Bible,' I said. As we'd
walked I'd been hoping the Bible thing was a mistake, maybe
a bizarre homework assignment. But Christopher just stared
into the distance. 'Tell me, why is it that Christians always
have to wear Jesus on their foreheads?' I asked, feeling
horribly cranky and tired and stupid for having wasted over
an hour getting my hopes up for nothing.

'I see you know a lot about Christians,' he said, bending to
rub Gal. His voice was sarcastic. He looked up at me and his
eyes were sad, proud, full of secret things. My anger vanished.

'I know enough,' I mumbled.

The bus appeared in the distance. 'Well,' I started to say –
meaning goodbye, but instead my fingers brushed his, his face
moved toward mine and we were together, hanging in each
other's arms and our mouths sealed tight, holding on for what
seemed like forever.

I gave him my number and all the way home tried to decide
which was worse: if he didn't call or if he did. His tongue had
touched mine like a spark. The heat went out in rings. When I

thought of his kiss my chest burned, like I'd been scorched.

The bus pitched in traffic and my hangover came back, and then memories of the Pig's party – the basement so loud and crowded and too much beer, too much beer … the bedroom tomb-dark and rocking, heaving, with the Pig's fingers like bugs under my clothes, waking me, forcing me up and out into the hall, my stomach stewing and the music cranked to pure pain. As the bus huffed and fumed at a backed-up traffic light, I started to cry. Too many things were inside me: smoke and booze, whispers and wailing guitars, faces, fingers and tongues. I wasn't even legal and I felt a hundred.

Back then, I hadn't had a real boyfriend yet. Almost seventeen and never had a real boyfriend, just guys who I'd have crushes on and date and get dumped by after a few weeks. Or guys at parties, guys you have a beer thing with, the one-time gropey thing where you pretend nothing happened come Monday at school. Or the friendly thing, where you're basically buddies and stuff only happens when you're both tanked because there's no one else and it's nice. You still pretend it never happened later. The Pig thing was different. The Pig thing was A Really Bad Night.

At home I felt too wrecked to even play my new copy of *Undercover*. I slept, then ate, slept then ate, then felt good again. I ignored my dad's notepad message to call Regina. I didn't want to go anywhere or have anything else happen to me. I was supposed to be sick with the flu anyway. My parents went out after dinner and I lay on the rec room sectional in my pyjamas with the TV on low, thinking about religion and God. When the phone rang, I didn't pick it up.

No one in my family is religious. The only copy of the Bible in

our house sits in the rec room on the bookshelves that contain
Dad's beer stein collection, *National Geographics*, their
university textbooks and other winners like *How to Curl Like
a Pro* and *Old Railroads of Ontario*. Mom once told me that
one of our ancestors built a church near Kingston and it's still
there. But in those days, she said, everyone believed. 'Is God
real?' I'd asked her. She said it was something I had to decide
for myself. She believed in God for a couple of years once, but
stopped when her dog got smucked by a truck. So I'd talked
to my dad, who began cleaning his glasses with a crumpled
Kleenex and said he'd gone to church when he was a boy,
though only because they had to. 'But you got married in a
church,' I pointed out. He said only because they had to.

I did know about Christians, though, because in grades
seven and eight I went to Pioneer Girls, a kind of Girl Guides
for God lovers. We met in the basement of Greenview's
church, a small, scab-brown building beside the variety store,
with yellow frosted-glass windows that look like they belong
in a bathroom. I started going because Bono did and it was
something to do back then on Thursday nights, I guess. The
group was run by neighbourhood ladies, who made us stand
in a circle holding hands at the start of each meeting and sing
this song, their anthem:

> *Pioneer Girls, across the prairies*
> *In the days of wagon trains*
> *Pressing on with sense of purpose*
> *Scaled the mountains, crossed the plains.*

We read the Bible and did crafts and held hymn
singalongs. We wore uniforms that were blue jumpers with
red sashes across the chest and matching blue-and-red hats

..............................................................

called beanies. The ladies were worried about our souls.
*Pioneer Girls: Turning Girls to Jesus,* the Badge Activity Book
said. The ladies were nice until you laughed or said bad
things like What about evolution? What about carbon
dating? Which I started to. Then Mrs Tromblay would come
over. Enormous, swaying and sweaty, she wore pink lipstick
the colour of bubble gum, which made the wet black hairs on
her upper lip even more noticeable. 'You need to *calm down*,'
she'd say, staring into my face with her fat-pinched blue eyes.
A warm, dimpled hand pressed my shoulder as she bent
closer. 'Do you under*stand*, Germaine?'

After Bono and I got kicked out of Pioneer Girls we would
visit the church Thursday nights, hovering by the basement
windows. When the singing stopped we'd scream CHRIST
ALMIGHTY SAVED ME, blast a few snowballs, and take off.

Lying in the rec room with the Bible in my lap, I thought
about telling Christopher this story, if he called. And if he
didn't, I would tell Regina the story of how I kissed a
Christian. The fiery lump in my chest was still there, but it
was cooling. If I hadn't answered the phone – it was ringing
again – maybe it would have gone out for good.

'Got a light?'

Yeah I know, the worst line in history, but it's useful.
Except that Imposter Boy's clueless. He just blinks, his beer
paused halfway to his mouth. Up close, I can see there's a
mean look to his face. The difference between him and
Christopher is even more obvious. Still, he's good looking.
And there's a trace.

'Sure,' says his smiling friend, whose thin frizz of hair
under his baseball cap makes him resemble a small scarecrow.
Instantly his Bic's under my nose, one hand cupped gallantly

to protect the flame. It takes a few seconds longer than it should for me to light up because my hand's unsteady, either from nervousness or drunkenness or both.

'Thanks.' I smile quickly at friend, then grin up at Imposter Boy again. Nothing.

I drag on my cigarette and nod to the music, which is just rhythmic noise this far from the house. I catch myself fluffing my hair and stop.

'So, how do you guys know Casey?' I ask.

'Who's Casey?' says Scarecrow.

'The one having the party.'

He sticks out his bottom lip. 'Don't know the guy.'

As if this is funny, I smile yet again at Imposter Boy, who's really irritating in the way he continues to watch the crowd, his buddy, or an empty point in space. Daniel says I'm beautiful. I love you, he says, stroking my hand, rubbing his nose against my neck. Beautiful. Yet whenever I start to believe it, someone like Imposter Boy lets me know it's pointless, the eye of the beholder's not reliable, ever.

I try once more. 'Hey.' I raise my eyebrows at him. 'How'd you like to get high?'

Imposter Boy's eyes shift, click on my face.

Bingo.

Christopher wasn't just religious. His father actually ran a church out on Main Street East called the Holy Annunciation of Ebenezer. He'd once been a priest. Now, from the sounds of it, he was a wacko. Christopher had six older brothers and sisters and shared a bedroom with two of them. His high school, called Wellington Christian Central, was a freak unit of only three hundred kids. Families had to donate money to keep it going.

'Do your parents make you go?' I asked.

'It'd be hard not to.'

'But do you like it?'

'Sure.' I almost hung up then. 'I mean,' he went on, 'it's school, right? Do you like yours?'

'Fuck no.' We laughed. I told him about MacKenzie. 'It's a school of the bored and the damned,' I said, 'but I'm one of the saved.' What the hell was I saying and why did I talk like that? I described the hordes of preppie girls in Daniel Hechter sweat shirts and pastel hair bands, the ones Regina and I outrage with sex and drug talk. I told him about my wild friends on the smoking pit who sell hash oil and bennies and orange microdot and how we all get fried and have a laugh riot. I claimed I could quaff a six-pack and still talk normally to my parents, that Regina's nickname was Blowjob Queen (though it's not exactly true). I wanted Christopher to freak out and scamper back to his Jesus puff in the sky, but at the end of the conversation I said, 'So, do you regret kissing me?'

He asked when he could come over.

When I told Regina about Christopher she squealed about how 'adventurous' I'd been, picking up a guy downtown, and then she demanded complete physical details: appearance, hair length, butt cuteness, body parts groped and fondled, probable or confirmed cock size. Finally I said, 'The only problem is, I think he's a Christian.'

Her eyes bulged and she almost spewed a mouthful of Slurpee. 'Yikes! Like, how much of a Christian?'

'I don't know. His parents are total Bible thumpers. It might be mostly them.' I wished we weren't walking through the church parking lot at that moment, cutting to Glenacre

Street from the variety store. The chapel was dark, but I still
didn't like being near it and remembering that I once was
inside, wearing a jumper and crocheting Jesus Loves You
place mats with Mrs Tromblay.

'So has he tried to convert you or anything?'

'Fuck no!'

Regina grinned. Possibly to cover her freckles, she'd
recently started wearing thick foundation a shade whiter than
her skin. In the parking lot's dim light, with her teeth and lips
stained Slurpee blue, she looked ghoulish. I shivered. 'Are you
sure?' she asked. 'Not even during a moment of passion?'
And she threw her head back and panted: 'Oh Germaine ...
cum with me to Jesus ... grasp the rod of God ... ah, oh ...
oh yes, oh yes ... yes suck the cock of ages, now OPEN YOUR
THIGHS TO THE KINGDOM OF THE LORD!'

Her screams trailed off to yelps and groans that
reverberated through the foggy night, but I hardly heard
them. What I mean is, I forgot they came from her. *Ohhh.*
How when I'd pressed my hand between Christopher's legs
he'd let out a long low moan, an animal cry like I'd never
heard. Making out on the rec room couch with my parents
gone, his hair brushing my face, it would have been obvious
even if he hadn't told me that he'd never had a girlfriend, his
mouth was so unsure. But not for long.

Even though it was a school night, I took my time walking
home after Regina left, because late evening is the only time I
like Greenview. In the dense mist like suspended rain, the
dark houses seemed to recede. Down the street the electric
lamps on lawns shone from invisible posts, a constellation of
cloudy moons. The city's distant echo was a faraway moan.
*Ohhh.* My head was filling up with Christopher Weir. His mouth
was in the dampness, his scent in the stirring breeze. I felt

weak, a dandelion puff that can barely hold its shape, that's already pulling apart, spreading itself into the waiting air.

In my head, I talk to people.

My brother Ian once told me he believed in the quark, which is as powerful as God. 'But you can't talk to a quark,' I said. He screwed up his face.

'Why do you need to talk to it?'

But I have to talk to someone, or I'd go insane. When I was really little it was an imaginary friend named Joe, a man I once saw hosting a fishing show on TV. Nobody important, just my friend Joe. Later on, down by the river in the ravine, my friend was the Indian man who used to own the arrowhead that I keep in my room. He was a great person to talk to. He'd been around long before Greenview existed, and he agreed that my school and teachers and snotty classmates were all just a pile of shit. All the twisting crescents, all the driveways regular as integers, all the brush-cut lawns and Doulton-figurine living rooms frozen in perfection and all the dead dead dead-end days of scuffing around the neighbourhood looking for something, *anything* to do – in time this would all vanish, he said.

Christopher was coming over on Tuesdays, my parents' Scrabble-club-out evening, and also on Friday nights, which is curling. I showed him my room. Mattress on the floor, fancy dresser set covered in scarves, wine-bottle candleholders and psychedelic light bulbs and concert posters with feathered roach clips dangling from their edges – Christopher looked carefully and expressionlessly at everything, like he was peering into a totally new world, and for the millionth time I thought: This is crazy. I also thought: Nobody's ever been this fascinated with me.

## Bread and Stones

Each time he visited I was terrified someone would see him walking down from the Glenacre bus stop, Regina or one of my other friends out roaming. I could imagine the conversation:

Regina (looking him up and down, especially down, and grinning hugely): 'Hey! You must be Chris. Germaine's told me *all* about you.' Then, noticing that goofy football jacket he always wears (probably inherited from a nerdy sibling): 'Wow, cool jacket man. Hey, it's not a Sabbath jacket is it? I thought I saw something like it at the concert.' (There was no concert, Regina doesn't even like Black Sabbath, but that's not the point, and Chris would be left puzzling over what on earth a 'Sabbath jacket' could be.)

I was reading the Bible. The Gospels, actually, which is the only decent part because Jesus was such a rebel and a hell-raiser – something I find endlessly funny and pathetic, considering the straight-assed losers who follow him. Chris and I talked on the phone every day. He still didn't say much about his religion, but we talked about everything else, it seemed, and he read a poet named Yeats to me in an Irish accent that he learned from his grandparents. He told me about spending summers on their farm in Kerry, about riding a horse through wet fields. I pictured him on the horse, his pelvis rocking in motion, unaware of his loveliness. I told him how years ago I'd found the arrowhead deep in the ravine, that if it wasn't for the ravine I'd die of lawn monotony out here, that I had a collection of river rocks imprinted with fossilized leaves and skeletons of insects and ancient crayfish, that I loved to think about Greenview being all swampland, with these creatures silently moving through the water. Every time Christopher and I talked it got harder to remember that he was a Christian freak who my friends would despise. Who I despised.

'Does he party?' Regina asked.

'I don't know,' I lied. Then added, 'He lives downtown,' as if this might be something.

Regina wasn't impressed. Chris and I had been together a few weeks and she was starting to act annoyed. I hadn't brought him out with our friends, like I'd promised. I hadn't even introduced the two of them.

'So, what's he like?'

'How?'

Regina exhaled a cloud of smoke. 'In the sack!'

'Oh.' I giggled. My fingers touched the chain-link fence and curled around the wire. Over on the smoking pit, some of our friends blinked sleepily at us as they pulled on their cigarettes.

'They can't hear us,' Regina said.

'Yeah. Well, he's good.'

'Yeah?

'Yeah.'

'Like, orgasmic good?'

My grin tightened. 'Uh, no. Not that good.' No one I'd met was that good. Even Regina had only had one who was that good. Christopher's kisses were long and deep, but when (after waiting through a few sesssions on the couch for him to do it) I finally put his hand between my legs, he'd gone completely still as if stunned. We lay rigid for a long, awful moment when I thought he was going to pull his hand away. Slowly his fingers began moving, gently pressing down on my pubic bone through my jeans, pressing carefully like I might break, pressing, pressing, until at last, embarrassed that he couldn't or wouldn't do anything else, I shifted my hips away.

Regina put on her proper lady voice. 'And have the two of you indulged in sexual intercourse?'

'Right!'

I took her cigarette and put it in my mouth. 'Well?' She widened her eyes. 'Would you? Will you?' I hadn't 'indulged' with anyone yet, but Regina had, six months ago with Mr Orgasmatron and with another guy since. I was falling behind.

'I'm considering,' I said. And maybe because I knew Christopher was the only guy who'd never push it, who might even refuse to do it, I realized that I wanted to, with him. A scene came to me: he and I in a tent or little cabin by a river, woodland stillness around. Lying naked on wool blankets. Naked and unseen.

At school I'd dream about Christopher for entire classes, then suddenly snap out of it, recalling where I was (MacKenzie Secondary, with a ball of hash in my pocket) and where he was (Bible Screamers High, with parables of Jesus playing cards in his). On the smoking pit, in front of our friends, Regina cackled that I had a secret lover, a lover of God. God? someone said, looking alarmed. I gave Regina the eye. 'She means godlike,' I said, and lit another cigarette.

I finally pinned him down on the whole believer thing. Or tried to.

Do you believe in Noah's Ark? No answer.

What about heaven and hell? Yes.

Do you believe God listens to your prayers? Yes.

Should everyone be a Christian? No answer.

Do you believe rock music, say by the Rolling Stones, is a sin? No answer.

Heaven and hell my ass. It's so embarrassing, God like a principal damning people to eternal detention. Who needs more of that crap? Christopher said God wasn't like that for

him, that he was a friend, but I think then that he was
making up his own version of God, and if you're going to do
that why sing the marching songs and blab about damnation
and salvation with the rest of the brainwashed? He called me
prejudiced. I called him a baby. There was silence on the
phone, and just then someone at his house picked up the
extension and started dialling. Between the clicks of the
numbers came Chris's voice saying *hang up*. I knew he
wasn't talking to me, but I did.

What did he think? That we'd just keep meeting in my
basement, talking on the phone? The Friday nights I was with
him I was missing parties, of course. Regina would call and
taunt. I'd make up lame excuses she didn't believe.

We were lying on my bed in candlelight. I'd unzipped him
for the first time, my fingers reaching inside his underwear.
He gasped, then pulled away.

'What?'

He rolled on his back then faced me again. 'Nothing.' He
smiled and touched my hair. I stared at him. *Please don't
embarrass me.*

'You just don't waste any time,' he finally said.

'What are you talking about?'

'Nothing!' He laughed and kissed my forehead. His cords
were still parted, revealing a white peak of underwear. He
kissed me again and wrapped his arms around me, but all I
could think of was that carefully loosened zipper and my
hand trying to slip inside, and how this had been stopped,
thwarted, like I was some kind of pervert.

'When can we get together again?' he asked later. He put
his nose to mine and bounced on his toes, still the eager
puppy.

'How about Sunday morning?' I smirked. That calmed

......................................................................

him down. After a minute I added, 'This is stupid.'

'What?' His brow creased and his mouth hung open. He'd
been so enthusiastic about us the whole time, like nothing –
not the unholiness of my room or my stories of wasted
weekends – fazed him, made him hesitate. Now he looked a
little stunned, like he was finally catching on. I could see he
didn't think it was over, but the belief that we'd go on had
been given a jolt. It was cracking.

He would blame me.

'You should have a different girlfriend,' I said. 'Someone
from your school.'

He glared with hard, moistened eyes. 'Really? Why should
I do that?'

'For fuck's sake, Christopher ...' I sighed and swept my
hand around my room. I didn't know what else to say.

Christopher once told me that in his church, anyone could
stand up and preach. He'd done it himself. It wasn't really
preaching, he said, just talking about what God had done for
you. When Chris spoke like that I had no idea what he was
saying. God this, God that – all this God talk and no one
really knows what God is, they just read the Bible like it's
obvious, learn the passages like a fucking exam. 'I am the
way, the truth and the life,' the Pioneer Girls ladies droned.
But what did that have to do with Mrs Tromblay's hand on
my shoulder, with bright pink lipstick?

I couldn't end it right away. I saw him once more and said
nothing, then afterward wrote him a letter, a short one. Talk
about a cop out. I looked up his address in the phone book,
then got an idea and borrowed my mom's car.

The house was a plain brick bungalow on a dark side
street downtown. I drove past, parked, and walked back.

Heavy taupe curtains blocked the front windows. I cut across
the lawn to the side, where light shone from the basement
windows. I squatted. In the first room, a woman in a cotton
dress with her hair tied in an elastic was folding laundry. The
only woman I've seen doing housework in a dress is my
grandmother. Grimacing, I wondered if this was another
religious rule, a bizarrity Chris hadn't told me about. There
were likely tons of creepy details he hadn't admitted. Feeling
better about the envelope in my pocket, I shifted over to peer
into the next window.

Christopher, fully clothed, was lying on his bed.

I sprang back, heart thumping, and crouched on the cold
grass before crawling forward again. The wood-panelled
room was tiny, like a summer-camp cabin except without the
graffiti. A bunk bed stood against the far wall, a regular bed
in one corner. Chris lay on the bottom bunk with his arms
behind his head, staring up at the bed above. His eyes were
black and unmoving. One patch of bare skin showed where
his shirt had come untucked from his cords, another at his
throat. I remembered kissing him in both places the last time
we were together, inhaling his clean sweat smell, dunking my
nose in the hollow of those collar bones. And later, being
dazed that I'd done this when I was already looking forward
to him being gone, to phoning Regina and saying 'What's
happening Friday night?'

*Dear Chris*, my letter began. Awful, stupid. I wrote: *You
believe you know me, but you don't.* His eyes stared at the
underside of the wooden bunk, stared like he was looking into
the universe. Can you love only a part of someone? Aren't you
supposed to take the whole? *I'm not like you think.* But how
does the part fit into the whole? And what do you do when
one part seems big enough to be a whole in itself? I'd been

clear when I wrote the letter, and even two minutes ago, but those moments didn't relate to this one at all. 'Christopher,' I whispered, and as if in answer Gal trotted into his room and barked. Chris's eyes jumped to the window. I fled.

I'm back in the house looking for Daniel, who has dope. Stereo speakers maxed on Hendrix and there seem to be a hundred people on the main floor, hundreds in the yard – every partier from the north end must be here. The dining room's like the top of Hash Mountain, with shadowy figures preparing bottles or giggling quietly in the murk. I spot Daniel with some of our friends, his slim body leaning against a wall papered with what looks like a pattern of trophies or urns with flowers. When I approach he gives me a red-eyed grin and slides an arm around my shoulders. Daniel, my first real boyfriend. I run my palm across his bum, reach into his jacket pocket and remove the plastic baggie. His hand lingers on my shoulder, tries to keep me there as I move away, mouthing *I'll bring some back.*

I stop at the truck for more beer, then lean against the bumper and watch the crowd. Glazed and dopey faces, some girls stumbling with sloppy smiles. The bonfire's startled snap and a waft of smoke. Daniel's touch has stayed on my shoulder, his eyes saying don't go. I know I can't return to Imposter Boy. I'm drunk, but not that drunk. I cannot try to pick up a guy with my boyfriend's dope. 'With my boyfriend's dope!' I say aloud, smirking. Tears fill my eyes and as I look at the ground it seems to whirl, a darkness waiting to swallow me. I am terrible, I think, my cheeks burning and wet. I deserve nothing.

Sniffling, I skirt the crowd. Hug the shadows alongside the house, the farmhouse that no longer has a farm, just scrub

fields and a slanting barn. In the pasture beyond the yard,
rusty pickups and skeletal cars lie like the remains of long-
dead cattle. I walk among them now, slowly, the ground
unpredictable here, brambles grown thick around window
frames, over half-buried humps of discarded tires. The party
gets quieter and I start to hear other things: cars on the road,
wind swishing grass. My shoes crunch on the ground. Ahead,
the barn door yawns. I peek inside, shiver. Turn and slide
down the wall to the cold bare earth, then pop a beer.

He never called after he got my note, mailed days later
when I was feeling sure again. Sure enough. But he wrote
back. Sometimes I reread the letter. It says that I have the
love of God in my heart, but am turned away from it. (First
problem: I have no idea what he means, but I think he
equated love of God with love of him, Chris.) It also talks
about destiny, that he won't tell me what to do because he
believes we all follow a destiny set by God. (Second problem:
I think he was actually hinting that my destiny is to be with
him, Chris, which will never happen.) The only right thing in
the letter is that he says he knows I won't like to hear all this.

From the barn, the people at the party are faceless,
silhouettes against the house lights and the fire. The barn's
rotting, it makes creaks and pops. Maybe it'll collapse on my
drunken idiot head.

If I were a real pioneer girl, I could have married
Christopher. A church wedding, in my relative's church.
Chris's father reciting the vows. It would have been normal,
then. But that was a long time ago, and the only god I believe
in is like those grey clouds lit by tonight's hidden moon, and
the sharp smell of my beer.

..................................................

# A Dirty Little Secret

It's definitely bad. Loaning me Mom's car for the weekend,
and if they notice the dent when I get back I'm fucked and
how the hell can I explain what really happened? They'll just
think I'm lying, and it's not too surprising why.

Could they be persuaded to think someone dinged them in
the grocery store parking lot? It's possible, if they don't notice
anything for a while. The greater the time, the greater the outside
possibilities, the better my chances of getting off. At least the
mark's on the passenger side, low down on the door. A triangular
stab streaked black. I hope that asshole broke his toes.

I'm so tired. And to think I was going to take off earlier
this afternoon, right before it started. I was getting ready to
go, then thought, why am I cutting out now? It's not like
there's anything to look forward to at home, except school
starting up again tomorrow. I'd been assuming I should leave
just because I wasn't drinking, which is kind of stupid, but I
was burnt, too. Three days' camping and partying, plus the
whole Daniel and Lisa thing – that wore me out a bit. Yet I
didn't leave early, I ended up being there for it, and now I
have to play chauffeur *and* deal with this damn dint while
Regina and these useless tools get to recuperate, forget.

Because I'm taking side roads. It's nicer.

Yes I do. The turn-off's after we pass 24. After Simcoe.

Use that thing, Todd. It pops up into an ashtray.

I have to remember to empty it. And this one. Mom finding a roach would just top things off.

Sundown when we pulled in. No lake, no woods, just a shadeless plain full of glinting metal. Perfect recipe for sunburn, sunstroke, sun madness.... The so-called campground looked like a Third-World ghetto: tire-track lanes, people with doughy, junk-food faces camped around their cars and vans in whatever space they can grab. Mountainous garbage drums with hornet colonies rising to fight you when you toss something in. For facilities, only those puny port-a-poos with their hot piss reek, and too few of them, so cutting between sites is a slalom through tent ropes and spoiled beer cases and men spouting unsteady streams of pee. The field itself totalled, worn to a hard white dust that burns – it might as well be concrete. Hot overhead, hot underfoot, and all around the cars are radiating heat like open ovens. Christ. We didn't even have a picnic table.

I was looking forward to it for weeks. Stuck at home all month because Mom and Dad decide we're not going to a cottage as promised, they just want to do some redecorating and relax in the garden. Thanks! Friday afternoon I finally get everyone loaded in the car and we lose the suburbs, score beer with Todd's fake I.D., pass the last tacky strip mall in Wellington and drive all this way only to pull into a car-crammed field beside a racetrack out off some concession. Total nothingland, ground zero – except for Wokoko, if you can call that blot something. Another scanty town in the farm land between home and Niagara Falls. A place you don't slow down for, and the lonely pedestrians scrutinize your car like it matters to them.

# A Dirty Little Secret

Whose idea was it to go there anyway? I'd never heard of Wokoko, Wokoko Speedway. What a hole! Engine noise all day, blazing hot, and I wasn't thrilled with the people either – like ones you see in the east end of Wellington, picking fights by the Regent Blues Bar or slouched inside the Always Donut. And no guy action at all, at least not for me, and Regina and I combed the place ten times over.

We should have just gone to Arbor Lake as usual. Look at that: my hands are still shaking.

It's on your right. Sticks a bit. No, go ahead.

The best part of this trip's been the drive. Look at that barn caving in on itself. It's so right, out here in the country. You can actually feel it, the rightness, wafting all around. The way the fields roll out to the horizon, calling you to follow. How the setting sun makes everything golden. Sky. The metal domes of silos. Fruit trees' yellowing leaves. Nothing crazy in any of that. The craziness comes from us.

Ha! And the big thing everyone was uptight about was how it would go with me and Daniel and Lisa there together. Everyone's been trying to keep us apart since we split, especially these last few weeks when Lisa came on the scene. I know it. 'Forgetting' to call me about parties or having them at the 'last minute' or not phoning me *or* Regina, which has got to be about excluding me. Or we do get together, but Daniel doesn't show. (Not that I blame him. I mean, what's the point once you've decided to hate someone? Me.) At first I thought he'd said something to make the others act this way, but now I don't think so. It's more like everyone automatically wants to ignore the uncomfortable. They don't even have to talk about it. I know how it works. I've seen it before. Oh no, they think, we can't have the two exes in the same room or the world will blow up.

Well. In a strange way, it did.

All the girls banded together and our guys, our supposed friends, cowering. Gone. I still can't believe it. Even Daniel: he wouldn't leave Lisa for a second, oh no! Had to comfort her while we got slaughtered. She was the only girl who didn't help, not that that was a surprise. I didn't think Daniel liked wimps, and after going out with him for over a year you'd think I'd know something basic like that. You really would think. How long does it bloody well take?

Todd, acting all serious, pulled me aside to tell me that Daniel and Lisa were planning to come this weekend. Slid his fingers around my arm near my breast, the weasel, and watched my reaction with big, eager-to-be-sympathetic eyes. As if I'd stay home! Even so, it did suck pulling up to the site with the two of them already there, leaning against Daniel's truck with their limbs entwined, loopy with love. Daniel, tanned and gorgeous as usual, looks at me in that vacant 'I don't know you' way he does now, then whispers something to her, *That's Germaine*, and like a child she tightens her hold on him, *mine mine mine*. Spare me. At least I'd never be so obvious.

Yeah, here it is. Can you pass the chips up?

Todd and Wayne are so quiet. Even Regina. Everyone's freaked out, we'd all rather be alone.

She's like a little girl, Lisa. The kind of little girl who used to drive me nuts because everyone thinks she's adorable and she knows it, she never has to worry about a thing. Doe-eyed. Great hair. God, she was practically screwing him in that lawn chair! Daniel and I were so not like that, so cool about not behaving like a couple all the time. And she didn't say a thing worth listening too, not the whole weekend. Hardly said anything at all, actually, and had this kind of hierarchy for

..............................................................

how she'd react to stuff. Like, when Regina made a joke, Lisa
would politely smile. When one of the guys did, she'd laugh
hysterically. When I did, she'd stare at the fire.

Friday night we're trying to settle in and have a party.
People from other sites are drifting up friendly enough, saying
Hi, where ya from, wanna buy/sell/smoke some weed?
Regina's chatting up a moustached dude in an STP Oil T-shirt
whose eyes are stuck on her boobs, as usual. Todd, Dave,
Scott, Bubba and Ken are spread out on the ground playing a
huge cross-firing game of caps. Jackie, whose nose is already
burned and peeling, has teamed up with Wayne and pushed
coolers together to form a joint-rolling table, while her little
sister Bea sits nearby, baby-sipping a beer and managing to
act pretty cool on her first trip with us. So everything's going
great – except it's not, because underneath we're all
pretending not to notice Daniel's truck, just beyond the
firelight: how it's shaking and creaking and practically
bouncing off the ground after he and Lisa have gone to bed
ridiculously early. Someone cracks a joke about busted shocks
but no one laughs, they're all trying not to watch me.
Shouldn't have looked, but how couldn't I? Now I'm stuck
with it, the image imprinted over all my memories of us: the
covered pick-up with its rectangular back window and
Daniel's silhouette inside, naked, raised on his hands. I know
exactly the expression and the sounds that go with that
moment. I know them better than Lisa. Funny, that. Like
watching a film of your life with someone else in your role.

Should watch the cigarettes, my throat's hurting. My head,
too.

Todd, not getting a reaction from me, let the cat out of the
bag: Daniel's really heavy on her. Heavy? Well, you know: in
love. Oh. So what did Daniel tell her, what story? That I'm a

heart-breaking bitch who dumped his ass for no good reason?
That he didn't care, that he loved me? Or does he keep that a
secret? How do you say 'I loved X until I started dating you'?
As if love can just up and find a new target.

What bugs me isn't that I want him back. It's this other
thing.

And all for a car race that wasn't even a real race. Waking up
Saturday morning to that sound. Waking up later, that is,
because I first woke up to the sound of my brain. Must have
been around seven and already hot. Regina's tent cooking, a
stench of old canvas and spilt beer. Rubber air mattress
plastered to my face and my poor feet stewing inside my
sneakers – which I'd passed out in, duh. DIE! DIE! GET
BACK TO SLEEP OR YOU WILL DIE! screamed Brain the
second I cracked an eyelid. DIE! DIE! TAKE OFF THESE
SHOES OR YOU WILL DIE! howled Toes. Brain won –
Brain induced more pain. Dehydration. Didn't drink enough
water Friday night, that was the problem. But how are you
supposed to remember to drink water when you're stoned and
drunk? That's the problem.

Around noon I heard the second sound in a dream. Yet
another prostitute dream, which seems to be the theme these
days. This time I was the prostitute. I was older, sitting all
dressed up in a gown at a long, laden banquet table with
other prostitutes and men in suits. We women sat on the
men's laps, and the men were loud and drunk. The one I was
with was very fat and wore a big diamond ring – I remember
this close-up of his chubby hand on my thigh, the ring band
dug deep into his finger. Soon he'll dig into me, I thought, but
I wasn't disgusted. I didn't feel anything. The man and I left
the table and went to a chandeliered bathroom to do it. When

## A Dirty Little Secret

......................................................................

he bolted the door I gathered up my dress and he was
suddenly close. His ring pressed the hollow of my thigh and
sent a shock to my groin, putting me right on the edge – but
then I heard it. I looked at the toilet and thought, what a
strange sound to be coming from that. Then I was wide
awake and listening, the sun a thousand-watt bulb through
the tent and my crotch crying out for the hand to come back.
Instead the sound came again. Short and deep, like a cannon-
fire thump to the air. A bizarre sound, though, not so much a
*pow* as a *whoosh*. Like a massive furnace, a dragon opening
his jaws and spewing fire.

Whooooooossshhh!

It came from all around, then silence. Wide-eyed and
shocked, I braced for a thunderous explosion.

Regina rolls over and mumbles fucking shut up without
opening her eyes. The world's ending and that's what she
says! Then all at once I notice voices outside talking normally,
the empty sleeping bags and mattresses scattered around me
in the tent. So it's not the end, no Godzilla raging through the
field with crushed cars in its claws when I poke my head
through the flap. No, just Daniel and Lisa, looking like some
magazine couple. How the hell does she keep her hair *boofy*
like that? And me with a swollen hangover face, probably a
seam line down one cheek, and yes, my unkissed, unpetted
body. Lisa knows it. She looks at me. She realizes what she's
got, how good her catch is, but what she can't figure out is
why I let him go. The man with a Greek god body now barely
clothed in cut-offs, the man with the covered pick-up that's a
travelling double bed, the man with the blond curls and sweet
face who's genetically programmed not to lie, who loves
giving oral sex and hugs, who said I love you and so obviously
meant it and showed it … who's fun and serious and

considerate and so much unlike the other lechers, posers, hosers, losers, users and geeks that it's amazing he fits in anywhere at all, but he does – everyone loves Daniel, you can't not. You can't not.

Yet it wasn't right. Whatever the hell that means.

Through the tent flap I see the baseball caps and sunburned shoulders of campers winding through the sites toward the track like they've been summoned by a higher power. Rippled, distant forms caught in an idling tailpipe's spew. But at our camp, the whole gang's clustered around the coolers looking grim because Todd can't find the bag of dope we paid into. Todd bitching that Wayne had it last, Wayne swearing he gave it back to Todd. Todd's harelip scar turning whiter as his face gets redder, and Wayne with his 'Goofus! Did you look for it?' and Todd with his 'No, asshole, I've just been sitting on my butt!' are just making it worse, then WHOOOOOOSH! drowns everything yet nobody flinches. When I finally make them shut up for a second and tell me what's going on I think the answer must be bullshit: a car burning jet fuel. That was the big deal. That's the noise, the grand attraction, the reason for the whole fucking weekend. A CAR BURNING JET FUEL. Not even a race! A thousand people camped in the goddamn Sahara to watch some guy nearly kill himself.

So they spent the days at the track. The guys, and Daniel with his Barbie doll. Can't imagine anything more dull. At least Regina agreed – she came to meet men, not car-entranced zombies – so we left Bea with the job of shading poor Jackie with a towel and went on tour, chugging beer that seemed to evaporate before it reached our heads. In the mid-afternoon, bored, our legs coated with dust to the knees, we

..............................................................

decided to visit the track. Just once, and it was enough.
We saw what looked like an amputated airplane. Take the
cockpit, shrink and flatten it a little, add wheels and two
great funnels on the back, fire it up and watch it quiver. The
contraption had to jerk toward the starting line. That was the
whoosh: combustion unleashed for a split second, like
pinching air from a balloon. BLAM! *Lurch.* Quiver ...
BLAM! *Lurch.* Quiver.... 'GO YOU MOTHERFUCKER!'
screams a guy in overalls beside me. Cretin. We're all idiots,
pushing our noses against the wire fence, the bleachers dark
with spectators on the other side of the track. And these
people, some of them are like, *forty*. Guys with grey hair.
Long grey hair of course, but still. Wearing he-man black
leather vests over pink bare chests that are either swollen or
sunken in all the wrong places. Down the fence I play
connect-the-spots with the bald patches. And with their
girlfriends, it's skunk hair: blond frizz and a beautiful black
stripe down the roots. Some have tattoos. They give Regina
and me witchy, eyeliner-ringed looks. At school we're the
ones labelled skanks, but at Wokoko we're the preppies.

The jet-fuel car shook so violently it was a blur, a mirage
from where we stood near the track's first bend. The driver's
brains must have been scrambled. Of course he created the
thing, actually spent his time doing that, so what does that
say? Probably that a dozen women tried to screw him
afterward.

Not even a race, for God's sake. Like those wind-up cars
for kids. BOOM, he blasts down the track in a screeching blue
fireball and then – poof! The fuel's used up and the car rolls
to a stop. Maybe two hundred yards and it's over. Talk about
premature ejaculation.

All weekend, apparently, it was the same shit over and

over, just different cars. Oh, sometimes they dragged, but only in a straight line down to the first bend. Whoopee. People still watched, and I know why – they were waiting for a crash. That's the real thrill. Like kids at school rushing to see a fight. Nobody ever tries to break it up, no one thinks of how it must feel on the ground, your body twisted, your face scraping cement.

People want blood.

At sunset, the guys staggered back to our site half-pissed and dehydrated, their eyes shining like they'd seen God. Lisa climbed on Daniel's lap and they necked while we tried not to look. As she got drunk, she started getting bolder. 'I don't want you to wear *hers*,' she pouted, plucking at the gold chain I gave him, which he still wears. Everyone's eyes shifted to me in the firelight. Will we have a show or won't we?

Yes, Tillsonburg. Jesus, Todd has to announce every place we drive through. And then say what he knows about it, which is nothing, or just say his usual comment: 'Huh, that's a funny name.' Everything is odd to him, everything but home. And nice he can just slouch in the back seat there with Wayne, acting like nothing's happened. What does he have to worry about? He's not driving a banged-up car home to his parents. He didn't fight a fucking battle. Oh God, what a pathetic lot! Shit for brains!

There seem to be two kinds of men in the world. Mellow guys like our friends, who are great to hang with or sleep with but are useless when something happens, as proven in technicolour today. Then all the rest, who are assholes in varying degrees. Who want to be kings and gods. The degrees exist only because some do it better than others.

These chips are gross. I ate too much crap this weekend.

## A Dirty Little Secret

..................................................................

Everyone was worried about a scene between Daniel and
Lisa and me. Ha!

It started so fast. Like an air raid from the blue, a guerrilla
attack. How long was he there, twenty minutes? Ten? Once it
started it seemed to last for hours, but it couldn't have, else
eventually people would have done something. Those ones
who showed up at the end, maybe. You'd think. But Dermot
and those guys, when I ran to their site and asked them to
come help, they didn't even answer! Unbelievable. I mean, I
could understand it, sort of, if they didn't know me. They're
from another school and not close friends, but they were the
only other people there from Wellington who we knew, and
we've partied together. I thought they'd leap up and roar to
our aid, be enraged. *Men don't hit women*. Were they just
stoned? But it was more than that. It was like they were all
embarrassed. Dermot, that turd, just looks at his beer. You'd
think making out with someone would count for something,
even if it was years ago. Ten or more guys we could have had,
if they'd have come, and NOTHING.

Sure, thanks.

The third time Todd's offered me a smoke. Definitely
feeling some guilt.

You'd think there'd be a reason. Something we did or the
way we looked. But he just came over and started, like he'd
radared in on us – bleep-bleep, sitting ducks ahead. As if he
saw right away what I've totally missed: that we're not a team
at all.

Still, it's better to have a reason, isn't it, when someone
tries to kill you?

I don't remember him arriving. Where was I? Early
evening and I'd decided not to head home until sunset. The
'races' over and we were all there. Jackie in Regina's tent still

165

hiding from the sun, Regina and Bea there with her. The guys lounging under the tarp they'd rigged from a plastic sheet, sipping the last few beers and stroking their weekend whiskers. Daniel and Lisa lolling in coupledom. I'd walked to the can, noticed how the smoggy haze that had enveloped the field since Saturday seemed to be breaking up, the outlines of tents and cars sharpening in the late afternoon sun. When I came back, Wayne was sitting alone on a cooler by our pale fire, roasting a wienie. Wayne who Regina and I always tease because he's so huggable, inches shorter than me and with that shy grin. He'd laid out a bun beside him, mustard and ketchup already spread. It made me hungry. I saw all this at once and also saw a stranger standing on the other side of the fire. I assumed he and Wayne were talking and went to get some food from the car. Wayne told us later that just as he'd finished cooking his *first* wiener the guy had shown up, and without so much as a 'How's it going?' had walked over, lifted the meat off the open bun and shoved the whole thing end-over-end in his mouth. Must have burnt his fingers too, Wayne said later, but he didn't get mad at the hot dog stealer. Easygoing Wayne. Instead he asked the guy if he was hungry and offered to cook him another.

But the stranger didn't wait for it. He started muttering as I was rummaging for my food. My gut tightened. I knew instantly the guy was blind drunk, drunk and mean. He flung out an arm. *Fuckin' ass!* Almost toppled, swatting the air as if stung by ghosts. *Fuck!* He didn't even seem to see Wayne. *Fuckin' shitfuckin' ass fucker!* Working himself up, words sloshed together in a mouthful of drool. Like a rabid dog.

Damp, platinum blond hair and a dark tan. Not a big guy, but solid, paunchy. Maybe nineteen. Belly flab jiggling beneath the black Motorhead T-shirt, bum fleshy inside his

..........................................................................

shiny nylon shorts. So pissed he couldn't stop swaying – how did I not notice that before? And skinny-armed Wayne crouched absolutely still, cooking his wienie. The contrast was almost funny.

Then things went berserk.

I just gaped, I mean, I couldn't believe it when the guy went for Regina's tent. He must have heard female voices, because he just suddenly lurches over and disappears through the flap, spewing curses. A second's pause and then the girls are yelling GET THE FUCK OUT ASSHOLE! Screaming higher and more desperate as he doesn't and the whole tent starts shaking and straining on its stakes as somebody pushes somebody and backs hit the walls and I'm yelling *Guys, come quick! Come quick!* and only Todd, though he's not much bigger than Wayne, jogs up and into the bucking tent. Where are the other guys? Where's Wayne got to? I'm yelling for help and people are spilling out of the tent, Regina with a fist in the guy's hair, twisting him backwards so he punches out *bam!* on her shoulder and swings at Todd and everyone else, raking fingernail welts into Jackie's sunburned arm, still swearing so loud his voice is cracking, his lips are shiny with spit, and *where was everyone else?*

I saw Todd holding his eye with his face pinched tight and felt I had to do something, but what? I went over to kick out the guy's knees from behind but couldn't even get close because he was spastic, spinning around and around himself, stumbling, punching out at nothing. Then he stopped. Thank God, I thought, it's over.

We were panting, but the stranger was heaving, bent over with his hands on his thighs, his sweat-soaked shirt rucked up his back. Puke, I thought, and I'll kick your ass when you do. I concentrated on willing this to happen.

He looked up, zeroed in on me. I'd moved the closest.

'Ya fuckin' cunt,' he sneered, swiping his lips with the back of his hand. 'Fuckin' lousy cunt.'

I stared into his eyes, the irises like oily puddles. I couldn't look away. Looking away would be some kind of admission.

'BITCH!' Spit landed on my arm.

Blood rushed to my face. *Say something, do something,* but what can you do when someone calls you a cunt? I put my hands on my hips and smiled the way my brother does when I do something stupid. Making that smile was so hard, like forcing a massive weight off my face.

I said, 'Boy, you're a real tough guy, attacking women.' I raised my eyebrows in awe. 'It must take a lot of guts to do that. Wow! I'm *so* impressed.'

That was my big speech. He didn't even hear it.

As soon as I started speaking he began swearing again. Crescendoing to a scream of threats – he was going to smash my face in, choke me with his prick, rip my cunt apart – take your pick – and all the time he kept grabbing his soft cock through his shorts and shaking it at me. He rocked on his heels, took a step closer, closer, the eyes drawing me in while I kept speaking loud and clear like I wasn't scared, putting new sentences together and hoping, hoping to find the right combination of words that would slip past the pollution in those eyes and find the small real part of him that could feel and think, maybe even be capable of good or want to be good, but not know how.

Funny how things seem. My mind's buzzing with adrenaline, we're locked on each other's faces, revving, and suddenly I notice a pair of sneakers lying nearby in the sun. Sneakers! White leather ones covered in grime, stretched and sagging around the mouth. Laces dirty grey. Amazing. Those shoes somehow seemed to be cancelling out what was going on. How could this be happening when they were lying there, the same as always? How can the world just keep going? It reminds me now of when Bono threw me into a snowbank two winters ago, on the way home from school, freaking out because I'd stopped hanging out with her, because I couldn't take her butch weirdness any more. My chin split open on a hunk of ice and I knew more was coming, but for a moment, when I opened my eyes, it was like I'd fallen into a white crystal world. So still. Our fight seemed distant, already over, all I wanted was to tell her, to show her this wonderful thing. Or something. Like war, I think. Like those Canadian soldiers battling on Vimy Ridge. How were they not distracted by the beauty of the day? By the rightness of that sky?

People don't think girls dream of being heroes but some do. I do. I'm sure Bono did. The Lisas just seem to want rescue. Yet I've always wanted to be rescued *and* save the day. But I couldn't do a fucking thing. Big tough chick, yeah. I backed off, lowered my eyes. Right away the stranger did something awful: he raised his face to the sky and yowled. That's when I knew appeal was impossible. He was insane.

Our standoff must have lasted only a minute. I looked around and saw that Regina, Jackie and Bea were still there with me, their freckled faces tense and sweaty. The yelling started up again. GET THE FUCK OUTTA HERE ASSHOLE! Our guys were nowhere. I ran around wildly and found Todd and a few others behind Regina's tent, saw a flash of Daniel and Lisa hiding behind his truck, spotted Wayne by my car. The rest had vanished from the site, and the remainder weren't even watching. *Anything* could have been happening to us. I ran up frantically and yelled at them to come, form a circle, then I ran over a few sites to where

Dermot and those guys were camped. I yelled at them over
the AC/DC screeching from a car stereo to come, please give
us a hand, and I didn't want to believe their sheepish faces so
I ran back to our site and saw nothing had changed, the guys
still hiding, the girls squared off in a line with their high
angry voices – Regina the loudest and scariest with her fists
raised to the stranger, who stood on wobbly legs, a grin
rolling across his face. Then craziness.

It was like he wanted to be cracked open, detonated. He
charged the girls but was too sloppy and only caught Jackie's
T-shirt. I heard a yelp and a rip and then he was off charging
Mom's car – booted the door like it was styrofoam, and then
he charged the goddamn *fire*. Punted the logs with a grunt, a
rush of bright embers and ash up his bare legs yet he didn't
flinch, grabbed the beer bottle Wayne had been drinking from
and RAH! winged it at Daniel's windshield. Burst of brown
glass and foam as he charged the truck, scaring Lisa and
Daniel into the open, and Lisa cried out and hung prettily on
Daniel's shoulder. And then, I'm not sure what happened. But
suddenly the guy had a tent pole in his hands and was coming
right at Daniel so I lunged and yanked it aside. Fucking
Daniel! He's stronger than any of us, the only good athlete,
and all he did was sort of flap his hands and back away. Lisa
screaming his name and being butt useless. God, how could
she?

As soon as I grabbed the pole the guy let it go, so it wasn't
like I did anything spectacular. Daniel's eyes met mine. For a
moment, it was like seeing someone I'd met in a dream. The
other Daniel, pre-Lisa, swam to the surface. And the other me
who loved him (or maybe just wanted to), she came up too. A
second chance, if I reached for it. Me and Daniel tearing away
in his nicked truck, churning gravel toward – what?

...............................................................

Engagement? An apartment after high school? Daniel's eyes
went blank, the moment gone like a stone dropped in water:
one glimpse, then it sinks forever.

What I want to know is where. Where does love vanish to?

When I looked around I saw flames reaching higher than
the roof of Daniel's truck. A burning log had rolled into
Regina's tent. People yelling *fire!* Wayne chucking food from
coolers and heaving the melted ice, others ripping out tent
poles, the tent caving to the ground and all of us stomping on
it to put out the flames. Then this calm descended. The freak
was gone. I thought I could see a patch of blond hair in the
distance, weaving toward the racetrack, but I wasn't sure.

So there we were.

One guy. We lost to one guy. But we never even played as a
team. All of us stood on the burnt canvas full of puddles, and
no one spoke.

Good riddance. Todd and Wayne gone, glad to be away from
Regina and me, no doubt. Well. I just want everyone out of
this car. Almost dark and tomorrow's school, my first day of
grade thirteen. I hope the ending's better than the beginning.

If we're not a team, what are we? All these years at
MacKenzie, the parties. Wasn't that a kind of love, like a
clan? Isn't that why we're friends?

The crowd came too late, people from other sites who'd
seen the fire, who wanted to know what had happened. 'I
don't know,' I told them. 'A guy came in ...' But I was crying,
so I walked away, retrieved my charred sleeping bag and
began to roll it on the ground. Regina was staring at her
wrecked tent as if there must be a way to save it. Or maybe
she was just remembering all the years spent inside, the two
of us in her back yard through the summers. The guys

bustled about cleaning up, muttering wow and holy shit, over and over. The crowd stood and watched.

See you tomorrow, Reg.

No, I don't think so. I'll take my chances. See you.

Telling Mom and Dad – what's the point? Another living-room tribunal, Dad pontificating about my poor judgement, their eternal disappointment. And I'd probably be banned from the car.

Galway Crescent. Here's everything just as it was three days ago. Neat houses all in a row, good children nestled in bed, and here she comes, folks, the bad seed, the sleazy, sneaking, car-wrecking chick who makes the neighbours stare and whisper, the weed in the fertilized lawn.

I know they're waiting with their lights and questions, but I don't think I'll go in just yet. It's good to sit in the dark, listen to the engine cool. Home, school – it's all another world. Everyone pretending the other thing doesn't exist. We just talk about what happens, dates when and countries where, but not where it comes from. Not why people decide to murder you one day – or love, or leave you to die. What this hunger is. Because no one knows, or if they do, they don't want to tell. It's a dirty little secret.

# Evolutions

## I.

The morning that a boy at school is arrested for attempted rape, Regina passes me a note saying that she's pregnant. Everyone in class is so excited by the presence of the police – two cruisers out back by the smoking pit's curb, another in front with the handcuffed boy inside, cops hulking by their cars, cops striding like cowboys toward the main office – that nice Mr Sullivan has already shouted twice and Regina's late arrival went unpunished. She looks like dog shit: puffy eyes, swollen, bitten lips, ratty hair. She wasn't on the pit during break, the hushed, nervous eruption of talk as the cops tightened their gloves and scanned the crowd, and when she slunk into class an evil hope rose in me that her lateness and appearance had been caused by some crisis with Daryl. It seems this is true, only not like I wanted.

Daryl. I still find it hard to believe that someone with the nickname 'Mutt' could turn my best friend into a love zombie. Or father a baby.

I reread Regina's note carefully, though it only has seven words: *I'm fucking knocked up. Don't tell anyone.* Probably the shortest thing Regina's ever written. At home, Regina's notes going back to our first week of grade nine fill four grocery bags in my closet. Sometimes we'd write several a

day, wedging them into each other's lockers or back pockets
between classes. Mine were short and boring, at first, while
Regina sent pages of foolscap, the gossip and weekend plans
mixed with hilarious, imaginary stories about people we
know, stories of criminal activity and sexual perversion with
cartoon illustrations busting the margins, tales like 'The
Adventures of Mr Fixler's Protruding Mole' that continued for
weeks in daily instalments. My notes back eventually got
longer and better, but they've never been as funny, at least
not to Regina.

I'm thinking of all this as gone because Regina hasn't
written for months, ever since she got serious with Mr Non-
personality last fall. She's gradually stopped calling, too. In
fact the only time I ever see Regina these days is between
classes on the smoking pit – if she's not occupied with Daryl,
who manages to show up an awful lot for someone who
doesn't even go to school here. I've become so used to
Regina's love trance that when I noticed Rob Alden (a.k.a.
'the Professor', our trusted note conduit) grinning intensely
and rolling his eyes to the floor as Mr Sullivan was at the
board, I just looked at him in wonder, thinking he'd had a hit
slipped into his milk box.

*Knocked up.* The words don't make sense. Regina's
supposed to be on the pill. We're all on the pill. What the
fuck? I write *How do you know? How long?* and signal Rob.
Regina gets the note, smooths it open on her workbook, but
doesn't write back. Trying to catch her eye is useless: she's
wearing a bulky turtleneck that practically swallows her chin,
and her permanently permed hair clouds her face. All I can
see is the chafed tip of her nose. When the bell finally rings I
call to her, but she just looks over her shoulder and says 'By
the courts after lunch. I'll meet you.' Until she's out of sight I

keep staring, elbowed and bumped by the hallway crush of
students eager to be somewhere else.

Andy Baker. Out on the pit, everyone's bug-eyed with shock.
*Andy Baker?* Booked on three counts of breaking and entering
with attempted sexual assault. Apparently, Andy Baker's been
prying open windows and surprising women alone in their
beds. They fought him off, every single time. Police traced
him to MacKenzie because, in supreme loser fashion, he
dropped his school ring at the last woman's house.

Andy Baker's in my grade and went to my public school. I
pass his house daily. He has a pasty complexion with blots of
beige freckles, and the most memorable thing about him is
that he makes a funny swallowing or gurgling sound when he
speaks, like Grover on Sesame Street. I didn't think Andy
Baker had even hit puberty, despite being in grade thirteen.
He's so tiny.

So much for my hope that this year couldn't get any
weirder. First the dent in Mom's car and bye-bye to four
months' allowance, now Regina's screw-up (ha ha) and a
psycho in our midst. Not to mention the hugely reduced ranks
on the smoking pit. Most of our friends left school last June,
took their grade twelve diplomas and burned out of the
parking lot blasting Alice Cooper. Only a few of us from our
group are enrolled in the five-year program. Of course,
everyone else is still here – the people who don't hang out on
the pit: the preppie hordes, the keeners and geeks, all busy
with university applications, attending recruitment fairs and
waving their brochures. The pit's still lively, but it's different
being the oldest and looking out on all the unknown faces
from the junior grades, who eyeball us shyly as if we're drug
lords and rock stars. I know how *old* we seem. I remember. I

once thought grade thirteen must be the most exciting year of
high school, but with six months until graduation it feels like
the long-prayed-for end's already happened. Is this all?

At the end of lunch I wait by the auto shop garage doors
for Regina. The doors are closed against the cold, muffling the
revs and shouts inside. I smoke a cigarette and watch the
snow falling in the tennis courts, which are wavy with deep,
unmarked drifts. I feel dreamy, like I'm seeing a movie about
my day. I think of Andy Baker the rapist, and then Regina the
pregnant teenager – TV characters. The first bell sounds, but
Regina still hasn't come. I head back to the pit, where a few
students linger under the low overhang, stamping their feet in
the cold. As I dash to class down the dangerously wet halls, I
get the horrible feeling (though I know it's false) that the
police have taken the wrong person, that it's Regina who's
gone, zooming on a one-way trip toward the dark blur of
downtown.

Jackie tells me later that Regina's gone home sick. I walk to
her house after school, with night falling fast and snow still
drifting down from a sky so bulky it seems to sag just above
the rooftops. Regina's face looms white behind the glass
before she opens the door. Though she's big-boned, today
everything about her looks fragile, even her old flannel shirt
seems about to unravel. 'C'mon down,' she mumbles, and
descends into the dim rec room. *Crime of the Century* is
playing low, the album we listened to religiously in grade
nine.

Regina flops on the sectional and covers her legs with a
blanket. After years of hanging out together every day, I've
not been over once since the fall. I sit opposite, dazed by the
lost familiarity of the room, of the house's smell. Regina lies

staring at the ceiling, an arm across her forehead. She looks
fleshy and soft and loveable. Questions tumble in my head,
but I feel I have to be careful, that I could easily push her
away.

'So,' I ask, 'are you actually *sick* sick, or more feeling-bad
sick?'

'I feel like shit,' she says. She watches her fists bunch the
blanket. 'I've been feeling like shit all week. Fucking Fixler
gave me the biggest hassle leaving today. I felt like vomiting
all over his desk. And then Mutt was supposed to come and
drive me home and didn't show. Did you see him?'

She looks at me briefly. I shake my head.

The problem's not just that Dope Brain isn't my type. It's
probably better that way – no clash, no chance of a crush.
But he's not *Regina's* type either. She and I used to like pretty
well the same guys. But gradually, Regina's boyfriends have
been changing, have been getting worse. And somehow
Regina has too. She's never given a shit who she shocks, and
this has always been a great thing because people around here
need to be shocked (God, do they need it). But Regina's
always been other things too: she's incredible at drawing, for
instance, better than most kids at school. Sketch books fill
shelves in her room, and the pictures aren't the usual boring
stuff: if there's a landscape, it's seen through a pond or a
cracked window pane. If there's a face, it's half-formed from
nails or vines or flies ... I don't know if she's still drawing, but
what she does do is dress slutty for parties now – I mean too
slutty, desperate slutty, in cleavage-revealing blouses with
tons of hairspray and face powder. You don't need to do that,
I keep wanting to say. *You* don't need to. And she laughs at
stupid, gross things, like Daryl's nickname for her: Sweet
Jugs. She actually laughs.

'So what happened?' I say.

'I'm fucking six weeks pregnant, that's what happened.'

'But how? What about the pill?'

She tells me she stopped taking it because of side effects: weight gain, bloating. She and Daryl were using condoms. I imagine Daryl fumbling with a condom – or rather, Daryl saying forget it to one. 'Like wearing a wet suit in a bathtub,' I heard a guy at a party say once. 'I didn't notice you were gaining weight,' I tell Regina. She doesn't answer.

Something thuds overhead. I nod at the ceiling. 'What do they think?'

Regina waves a hand. 'I have the flu.'

The phone rings, and Regina's mom hollers down. I know immediately when Regina picks up that it's Daryl: the way her voice drops to a whisper, her pouty tone. I squat by the stereo and flip through records while the conversation, which mostly involves Regina sighing 'yeah' – what happened to Regina the loudmouth? To Regina the teaser and joker? How did she get so *lame?* – goes on and on. I wonder why Regina bothered to tell me anything at all. I feel useless.

'I have to go. I'm supposed to be helping Dad with supper,' I say when she finally hangs up. Usually the mention of either of my parents will raise a smile and a comment from Regina, but she doesn't even seem to hear me.

I zip up my jacket. 'Call me,' I say. Then, suddenly afraid, I lower my voice and add 'So when can you go to the clinic?'

Regina won't look at me. 'I don't know yet. Mutt and I need to talk more.'

'About what?'

She sighs. 'He doesn't want me to get rid of it.'

A hard lump swells in my throat. For a second I can't say anything, just feel my fist connecting with Daryl's head.

## Evolutions

...................................................

'So,' I say, 'what does Daryl propose?' Although I try, I can't keep the sarcasm out of my voice. I sound like my Mom – that word 'propose', *What do you propose to do next year, Germaine?* But that's what happens when I picture Daryl, the dude who dropped out of school four years ago, whose friends have teeth stains and tattoos, who seems to know about fifteen words, one of which is 'widget', and who makes a living dealing skunk weed and collecting something called tungsten, which he melts down with a blowtorch in his parents' back yard and resells across the border.

'He thinks we should raise it,' Regina says.

God no!

'I think that's a little crazy,' I whisper.

Regina shrugs. 'I do like babies,' she says.

I walk home, homeward. Homeward and schoolward: a major part of my life.

Since kindergarten, I've gone to and from school with Jackie. But now that she has a boyfriend plus a part-time job, I'm usually on my own at the end of the day. Recently I calculated that I've walked this route almost ten thousand times, at least twice a day for thirteen and a half years. It used to take fifteen minutes to public school, and the time doubled when I started at MacKenzie (and almost doubled again when winter's unploughed sidewalks arrived). Except for schoolkids, the streets are always empty. Sometimes I see a man getting into his car in the morning, or a woman taking in the garbage bins. Other kids' parents. Sometimes they look at me: a cold, nervous, unhappy look. Dirty looks. I used to be freaked out by them, freaked out by the pure hate. But I've done enough snooping and listening to know that these righteous adults are worse than I've ever been, that there's no

one without a stupid, gross or evil secret. So now I just feel it,
the hate. I brush by its black fur and go on.

Around and around, I plod along the twisting streets, the
crescents and avenues and drives. The air's got that arctic
January bite – sharp in your lungs. The streets are thick with
ice and tire-packed snow, and cold soon creeps into my boots,
starts freezing my toes. Sometimes I think about how we're
just this package of flesh, of tender skin in a world of glaciers,
lightning bolts, metal. *Organic matter*, my biology teacher
says. Sometimes I don't know how we stand a chance.

Halfway home, across from the variety store's glare, I light
a smoke. Cigarettes make the cold a little better, though my
free hand gets numb. I turn past the church, then my old
public school with its yard of lumpy snowmen in various
stages of creation or disintegration. I pause in front of Andy
Baker's house (the windows are curtained and dark). Snow
drifts down. Flakes meet the wool of my gloves and
evaporate. All that energy going into each crystal, only to
vanish before it hits the ground. Like those millions of sperm
wasted by the pill, like the thing inside of Regina that has to
go.

That has to go.


Regina makes an appointment at the clinic, but she still says
she may not go through with it. At school we talk more now –
talk alone, I mean. But there's still this sense of being careful,
of not saying a lot more than we say. I tell her she can't have
a baby at eighteen, that it'll wreck her life. She says I'm being
hysterical, but I can tell she's scared. 'You won't be able to *do*
anything with a baby,' I go on. 'You'll have no *freedom*.'
Freedom for what, she wants to know – what couldn't she do?
And I don't really have an answer. I point out that she'd need

money, that a baby takes a lot of time, that she and Daryl
might split up and then she'd be raising it alone. But these
nightmares don't seem to bother her, and anyway they're not
exactly what I mean. 'You won't be able to go on the road
with me,' I say, suddenly struck for the first time with a vision
of our future after graduation: working for the summer, then
bussing to the West Coast together, having adventures. We
could stay at my brother's in Vancouver. We could do it. But
Regina just gives me a faint smile.

I guess I can't compete with Daryl.

Mutt Face drives up to the pit daily in his black van with
the teardrop-shaped side window. A round, turnipy face at
the wheel and the van chugging on for another half-minute,
in case not everyone has heard it. He climbs out slowly,
Kodiak workboots and his puffy vest unzipped even in
January. Taking his time, so Regina can come to him. When
they kiss, she clutches at his vest and he gives her a quick
rough rub, sort of like you would a pet you wanted to fuck.
They never smile at each other any more, not like at the
beginning when they would grin and giggle, and Jackie and I
would raise our eyebrows and look away. But now it seems
that the goofy love stuff was better than this seriousness,
better than acting like they're already parents. Regina hardly
smiles at all now. She has a constant, sad, elsewhere look on
her face, like all she can think about is Daryl, even when
Daryl's there. She's lost in another world alone. She's tumbled
down a leafy slope, she's drowning inside a flower, dissolving
without realizing that it's a trap. It's a bloody trap.

Love's like dope to some girls. You see it all the time, the
way they become these spacey, smiley things. Not Regina,
though – especially not Regina. More than any of our friends,
Regina was always different. Outrageous and awesome.

Having babies and getting married – that's what *everyone*
wants. Some of the preppies and geeks are already engaged
(seriously, it seems). They've got their whole fucking lives
planned, and guess what? They'll be clones of their farty
parents. It's like they can't wait to be old.

If Regina has Mutt's baby, the entire world will be
hopeless.

## II.

She does it! She goes to the clinic. The next day, pretending to
be concerned about how she's feeling, I can barely keep the
smile off my face. I want to celebrate. To top it off, Regina
and Daryl have had a big fight and split up. And instead of
being heartbroken, Regina's pissed off – finally. 'That prick,'
she says. 'Like I'm gonna have his baby when he can't even
remember to pick me up like he's supposed to 'cause he's over
at Chewy's getting stoned all morning.'

Daryl's no longer showing up at school, and Regina starts
to become her old self. For a few weeks everything goes back
to the way it used to be: we have sleepovers at each other's
places, we go to parties. We fool ID check for the first time
and see a Zeppelin tribute band at the Vic Tavern downtown,
where we drool over sexy Plant and Page look-alikes, then
sneak out before last set to catch the bus and escape two
bearded wonders from Owen Sound, who've bought us
pitchers of draft.

It doesn't last long. In the space of several days the world
turns inside out and sideways. Regina and Daryl reunite.
Regina has a major blow-out with her parents and decides to
move out, to in fact move out with Doorknob. At the same
time, with only months until graduation, she quits school. I
don't know the exact reason or even order for these events

because when she announces them to me on the phone and I don't agree that moving in with Mutt is totally awesome, she gets mad. She says I'm turning into my parents. Things are tense when we say goodbye.

During the following days, I can't help thinking about my premonition. Regina really is gone now – vanished from MacKenzie's halls and Greenview's streets like she never existed. In class her empty desk gets taken over, just like Andy Baker's was.

One evening I get out my class photos from public school. I want to look up Andy Baker, but I end up going through all of them. There's Regina, grinning like a little hell-raiser. There's me: grease-bomb bangs, fidgeting or looking the wrong way. And then there's Andy, his face a white smudge and every bit the skinny wimp. Was it all determined back then? In biology, evolution's shown as a straight line from ape to human. But my teacher didn't have anything to say about evolution *within* humans. Is this straight too? Is Andy the rapist the only possible version, or did something go wrong?

If the seed's there from the beginning, what if Regina's evolution is to be one of those saggy young mothers dressed in track pants on the bus? What if, maybe, she's not so different at all?

Greenview seems to have shrunk ten times overnight. I feel suffocated, choked by a short leash. On Saturday and Sunday afternoons I do the hour-long bus haul downtown. The department stores, the new mall, even the record stores I avoid because although I have my allowance again I'm still broke, as usual, I'm cashing in Christmas savings bonds to survive. Instead I read novels at the Tim Horton's or wander in the old farmers' market, a low-ceilinged building that

seems to be buckling under the parking garage built on top.
There's a coin-operated horse I used to ride as a kid, a pet
store with a twenty-four-year-old caged parrot named Sam. I
gaze at the stacks of produce in the merchant stalls, read the
Greek and Italian family names. I discover an ancient café
called Albert's where whiskery men drink coffee and a
cheeseburger plate costs three dollars.

Why am I so alone? It's not like I even know who I want to
be with. Slipping sunflower seeds to Sam (he takes them but
never eats when I'm there, his beak opening slowly to show a
dry, black, rubbery stub of a tongue), I try to imagine the
kind of person I'd like to meet, but everything is murky or
dead ends. I thought that once I started making cool friends,
everything would just keep getting bigger and better:
increasingly cool friends, increasingly cool parties and
boyfriends – evolution toward bliss. So when did it stop?

I've wondered if maybe I'm being punished. I've been
mean. I've been cruel. To my parents, who really aren't bad,
just dorks. And two years ago I did a really bad thing: I
dropped Bono, my second-best friend. I dropped her because
I was sick of her machismo, her teasing and gibing, the way
she always acted like I was a weakling she felt sorry for. Sick
of her swaggering walk ('Like an ape', Regina said) and her
boys'-only clothes. Christ, Bono was more guy than most
guys! But she was also amazing. The other stuff didn't matter
that much. The real reason I dropped her (cold: just stopped
speaking, calling ... fuck, I was awful) happened one day
when we were walking past the cafeteria, through the Gamut
of Eyes: benches along the wall where boys loiter in packs,
silently evaluating every girl who passes. I hate the Gamut,
hate getting my body fried like a bug under magnifying glass.
But worse than the burn was the fact that no one was asking

me out. Guys constantly looked, guys constantly made drunken moves at parties, but no one asked me out. Then one day, a day Bono was with me, I overheard a cute boy who was staring at me mutter to his buddy: 'Would be pretty good, if she wasn't with that freak.'

The end. Kaput. I suddenly couldn't stand to be with Bono any more.

Bono still hasn't made any other real friends. She's sunk to hanging with a couple of grubby boys who live on her crescent. I see them doing skids on the public school's tarmac after dark, hanging out on the smoking pit in their own small circle of baseball caps. She hasn't changed, and we both look away when we pass in the halls.

*Pretty good, if she wasn't with that freak.* But here's my favourite hangout, Albert's café, and it's full of freaks, freaked out, freaked to the max: bagmen and winos, nutbars, filmy-eyed widows ... the waitresses are pushing sixty and have pencilled eyebrows, jet black or platinum blond hair done up in buns. They'd probably crack gum it they didn't have dentures.

And then there's me.


Regina has a new phone number. It's waiting for me when I get home, scribbled beside the phone in Dad's handwriting. My parents always write down messages, but because I'm secretly a cruel person, I sometimes pretend not to get them. I don't know why I do this. More often I'm paranoid when the message pad's empty. Or teary, enraged, insulted, hopeless.

There's no answer at the number, so I decide it's time to go next door and get Jackie's opinion on the whole Regina situation. Other than acknowledging the bare facts, Jackie and I haven't said much about it. Not because Jackie doesn't

have an opinion – Jackie has paragraphs of often brutal
opinion on everything. But she's too smart to blurt things out,
knows how not to make enemies. And having a boyfriend's
made her nicer.

I squelch across the lawn and ring Jackie's bell. Her mom
answers and actually smiles. She's become nicer too, now that
she's divorced, now that she can have Al or Danny or
whatever gentleman friend it is over to the house for coffee
instead of sneaking around. Why did Jackie's parents wait so
long, I wonder, heading upstairs. What was the point of all
that lying, squabbling misery? Did they actually believe it
was good?

'Hey,' I say as Jackie's door swings open and 'Helter
Skelter' comes crashing out.

'Hey. How's it going.'

'Fine.'

I sit on the bed and look around, because it's impossible
not to. The walls of Jackie's room are covered in pictures.
*Totally* covered. Tacked edge to edge, posters, most of bands,
reach the ceiling and disappear behind furniture. The narrow
spaces above the window and closet are hung with concert
banners and flags, odd gaps filled with ticket stubs and other
paraphernalia. The door practically disappears when it's
closed, concealed except for the brassy knob protruding from
a carefully X-actoed circle in Mick Jagger's crotch. After years
of cutting and taping, Jackie's room is done. It feels much
smaller that it used to, and kind of haunted, like one of those
Egyptian tombs full of painted faces. I don't think I could
sleep here at night.

'Have you talked to Regina?' I ask.

'No.' Her face goes pinched, as if she's insulted. Maybe she
thinks that because Regina's more my friend, it's rude to be

asking Jackie about her. Or something. There are always layers of criticisms, innuendoes, tricks or plots packed into Jackie's words.

'Don't you think it's weird that she dropped out of school and moved in with Daryl?' I say.

I do it again. I say Daryl like DARYL, though I meant to sound neutral, to not taint Jackie's opinion. I mean, to not taint how she chooses an opinion to give me.

'You mean "Mutt"?' Jackie smirks.

'Yeah.' I smile back. Might as well have fun with it now.

Jackie shrugs. 'Well. Pretty stupid not to finish her diploma. I don't know why she had to do that.'

'I know.' We nod together. This is what I hoped Jackie would say. She takes off the *White Album* and puts on the Clash. Her boyfriend, who goes to school downtown, is into punk.

'But,' she continues, 'if Regina's not applying to university, she doesn't need her diploma anyway, right? She has her grade twelve.'

'But then neither do you. Or I. So we might as well both quit.'

Jackie crosses her bony arms, one hand holding each shoulder. Whenever she does this she looks invincible. So: she's decided to be unsympathetic, to not be scandalized by Regina's behaviour. 'I want my diploma,' she says. 'Doesn't matter if I'm not going to use it.'

'Did you know they've rented a basement apartment? It's on Dewry Street, right near the Mission.'

Jackie just shrugs. 'She probably would have moved out anyway, at the end of the year.'

I hadn't thought of this, and feel stupid. It's so obvious: why would Regina want to hang around Greenview? Why would anyone?

..............................................................................

'Are you moving out too?' I ask.

'I fucking hope so.'

'With Shaun?'

'Maybe,' she says, but her voice has gone tight. The question must be *too personal*. This is the way things get, when you have a serious boyfriend.

So everyone's leaving, everyone has a plan. Jackie, though she's always had great marks, wants to go full-time at the restaurant she works in. Regina is ... living with the Turnip. And I don't have a clue.


Did I endure thirteen years of desk-slavery to go back for more?

Did I sit through thousands of days of history, geography, biology, trigonometry, social studies, typing, music, art, sex ed., English, Latin and French to work in an oily kitchen breading cheese balls and chicken fingers?

The thought of university nauseates me.

The thought of a job chokes me.

My parents think I pulled up my grades the last couple of years so that I could 'do something'. On the phone to relatives, they say that I'm taking next year off. Really, I only did better to prove I'm as smart or smarter than the preppies. If I beat Annabel Lucas for the history and English awards this year, I'll be the only smoking pit rep on stage at commencement. This thought makes me giggle.

I'm hanging around the market one afternoon when I see a poster that says Summer Acting School for Youth. I always wanted to take acting, but the theatre teacher at MacKenzie's an asshole. I copy down the information and show it to my parents. They call the school, and before I know it I'm enrolled for six weeks in July and August. I'm not sure what

I've done. But at least I have my parents off my back for a
while, I don't have to find a job, and I'll have an excuse to go
downtown.

The end of May, and I'm writing in my journal one Sunday at
my favourite corner window table in Albert's café. I'm used
to being alone here now – I actually feel addicted to it, these
long weekend days with books, where other people don't
matter. Pot of tea, pack of smokes, a grilled cheese on the way
– and now Rob Alden, my and Regina's trusted note conduit.
I do a classic drop-jaw double-take at the person coming
through the door. The Professor spots me instantly and comes
over with his usual grin.

'Hey Germaine.'

'Wow, it's Professor Rob. Hey.'

'Can I join you?'

'Sure.'

Still smirking, he pulls out a chair. Quiet and amused:
that's Rob Alden. He unzips his nylon jacket. Underneath is
his usual nerd uniform: plaid shirt buttoned right to the
throat (in public school the collar was buttoned too) and
jeans that fit all wrong. I ask what brings him to Albert's.

'Oh, I hang out everywhere.'

I nod. This, of course, is bullshit. Rob does not hang out at
parties, on the pit, or anywhere cool. In fact, I've never seen
him outside of school. Keener, chess-club member, wearer of a
bona-fide bowl cut that makes him look like a British choir
boy, Rob got the name Professor from Regina and me in grade
nine, when he sat behind us in English and blew our minds
one day by standing up, his eyes twinkling, and reciting all of
'Jabberwocky'. Regina probably thought of the name – she
thinks of things like that, has a knack for pegging people, so

........................................................

what turned her Daryl-blind? Rob, though, has always had
something extra that made him unlike the other geeks. Not
just clear skin and better brains, but cool. A hint of it, a
whiff. Like he could become cool, if he tried, but just isn't
interested. Isn't interested in having much, in parties or
friends or chicks. Why is a mystery.

'Anyway,' Rob says, 'I spotted you coming in here, so I sort
of followed.'

We both grin at this, the idea of Rob trailing me, like a guy
who's interested would. Like a real guy would. But then I
remember Andy Baker, the boy who also seemed to have no
balls, so to speak, and my smile falters.

I peer into Rob's whorling green eyes. 'So why'd you do
that?' I ask, bitchier than I intend to. Rob flinches a little.
Pink blotches appear on his cheeks.

'To say hi,' he says.

The waitress brings my shiny sandwich and I dab out my
cigarette, feeling bad for scaring him. Rob hesitates at the
waitress's question. 'Why don't you get something,' I say, and
he relaxes, orders a chocolate milkshake.

How is it that, sitting at our sticky, butt-burned table, I
find myself slowly, over more pots of tea, cigarettes, a side
order of fries and a glass of milk, telling Rob almost
everything about these last months, telling him more than I've
ever told anyone? Posters and calendars cover the wood-
panelled walls of Albert's café, faded by decades of afternoon
sun. In the warmth of the corner table by the window, the low
voices of the men at the counter and the deep fryer's fire-pit
crackle, it seems that Rob and I are more like children again,
very young children, back when who your friends were didn't
matter. Except we have these memories. 'I never feel like
getting stoned or drunk,' Rob says. 'Life seems too weird as it

is.' 'Exactly my thought,' I agree, 'minus the stoned-or-drunk bit.' Life's too weird as it is. What will happen next? The waitress interrupts to tell us they're closing. We wait for our change silently, a little stunned. I can't tell what Rob's thinking, but I feel strange, no longer myself. My body seems to have expanded to become part of all this: Rob, the café. I still feel alone, yet differently. Why was I so upset all year? I can remember events, but they don't feel the same.

Outside we sniff the river-smell on the wind and turn toward the bus stop. The setting sun's reddening the brick buildings along Main. School's almost done forever, there'll be no more Monday mornings, no more back-and-forth. I'll have to go see Regina more, to be nice, but I won't let it get me down because who would have thought there'd be Rob Alden to talk to? I laugh out loud at this, the oddball pair the Professor and I make: rocker chick and grinning geek. Geek! But I feel no panic, rather a giddy newness unfurling: coming out of the buildings, faces, and sounds as we stride down Main, rushing out of the sky and fluttering through me until I'm full, surging with surprised joy.

The days to come, the infinite new days. Spiralling out from this moment in all directions, like at the beginning of the world.

I'd like to thank the magazines who have published my work, the Ontario Arts Council for a Writers' Reserve Program grant, and the staff at Porcupine's Quill for their hard work.

I'm grateful to the following people for their contributions to this book: J.D. Pipher, for his love and criticism (which he rightly believes are inseparable); my editor, John Metcalf, for providing a necessary kick in the butt early on and very useful comments and support later; Beth Easton, Eric Evans, Steven Heighton and Nick Power, for reading my work and providing astute feedback; Beth Easton and Mandy Pipher for their help with photography; and Chris Hiller, for her steady encouragement. I'd especially like to thank my parents for the confidence they've shown in my abilities.

Two stories – 'Thaw' and 'Clear Blue' – were first published in *Grain* and *The New Quarterly*.

'Clear Blue' is dedicated to David Lawrence.

JOLIE DOBSON

Sharon English was born in London, Ontario, where for a while she excelled mostly at memorizing song lyrics and episodes of *Star Trek*. She eventually studied English literature at the Universities of Western Ontario and British Columbia, where she dropped out of a Ph.D. program to pursue fiction writing. She currently lives in Toronto. *Uncomfortably Numb* is her first book.